LOVE LEAVES AT MIDNIGHT

The King came to Xenia's bed-side and looked at her luxurious red hair shining in the candle-light and at her tender lips, which were trembling because she was afraid.

"Do you know how beautiful you are?" he said.

Xenia knew the moment had finally come—the moment when she must tell him the truth.

"I love you!" he cried before she could speak. "I am wildly, crazily in love . . . I never dreamed I would feel like this . . ."

"I . . . have something to . . . t-tell you."

She felt him stiffen and slowly draw back.

Xenia took a deep breath. How could she tell him? she asked herself. How could she sweep the happiness from his eyes?

Bantam Books by Barbara Cartland
Ask your bookseller for the books you have missed.

Barbara Cartland's Library of Love

Barbara Cartland
Love Leaves at Midnight

BANTAM BOOKS
TORONTO · NEW YORK · LONDON

LOVE LEAVES AT MIDNIGHT
A Bantam Book / March 1978

ISBN 0-553-11751-3

Published simultaneously in the United States and Canada

Bantam Books are published by Bantam Books, Inc. Its trade-
mark, consisting of the words "Bantam Books" and the por-
trayal of a bantam, is registered in the United States Patent
Office and in other countries. Marca Registrada. Bantam
Books, Inc., 666 Fifth Avenue, New York, New York, 10019.

PRINTED IN THE UNITED STATES OF AMERICA

Author's Note

The Earl Granville, Her Majesty's Principal Secretary of State for Foreign Affairs in 1883, the year on which this novel is based, was a relative of my husband.

I have in my possession a passport signed by him for my grandfather James Falkner Cartland to travel abroad with his wife.

It is like a letter on very thin paper with the Royal Coat-of-Arms at the top and the Earl's personal one at the bottom beside his signature.

Great Britain was at this time and all through the Victorian era working continually through diplomatic channels to keep the balance of power in Europe.

Chapter One

1883

The train, which had left Victoria Station fifteen minutes late, was trying to make up time.

It seemed to Xenia that the carriage was rocking in a most unpleasant manner.

Although she had resented it at the time, she was glad now that Mrs. Berkeley had insisted on having the windows closed so that they would not be enveloped with black smoke.

Sitting opposite her employer, Xenia thought for the thousandth time how fortunate she was to be crossing the Channel and visiting France, not that Mrs. Berkeley let her forget it for a moment.

"Most young women," she said in her hard, rather grating voice, "would be thrilled to see the Continent of Europe, but in your case you are particularly fortunate."

Xenia knew this referred once again to the fact that she had been left penniless on the death of her father and mother.

While she had hoped that one of her relations might take care of her, it had in fact been a stranger, a woman who prided herself on her charitable impulses, who had taken her into her house.

1

The Honourable Mrs. Berkeley was the Squire's widow in the small village where Xenia had lived all her life.

Most of its inhabitants were employed on the Berkeley Estate, but her father had been the exception and she thought secretly that Mrs. Berkeley was resenting that she could not patronise him and her mother as she did everyone else.

There was, Xenia thought perceptively, something in the endless dispensing of her generosity that smacked of triumph.

It seemed impossible that Mrs. Berkeley, with her money, her large Estate, her magnificent mansion, should have been jealous of the quiet, unassuming Mrs. Sandon, who made no effort to assert herself in any way.

Yet Xenia knew her mother, unlike Mrs. Berkeley, was beloved by everybody who knew her simply because of her sympathy, understanding, and sweet personality.

Mrs. Berkeley had been determined to patronise the Sandons, and the fact that their only child was left destitute had in some obscure way pandered to her vanity.

"What would you have done," she asked Xenia over and over again, "if I had not taken you in and made you my companion, besides giving you a very adequate wage for the very little you do?"

This, Xenia thought, was unfair.

She found that in the position of companion to Mrs. Berkeley she was run off her feet from first thing in the morning to last thing at night.

There was always something to fetch and carry, there were always messages to be delivered, besides endless small duties that should really have been those of a lady's-maid.

Worst of all, there were the hours spent having to listen to complaints and criticisms not only of herself but also of other people.

Mrs. Berkeley was never satisfied. She expected

perfection but Xenia often thought rebelliously that she would not recognise it if she found it.

She had been desperately miserable after the sudden deaths of her father and mother from a virulent form of influenza which had swept the whole of England and had taken its toll even of the small village of Little Coombe.

A number of the old people had died, which might have been expected, but there were also children and even strong labourers, besides her father and mother.

It had all happened so suddenly and Xenia could hardly realise that she was alone in the world with nobody to care for and nobody to care for her.

Mrs. Berkeley, like an over-benevolent Fairy Godmother, had carried her off to Berkeley Towers, and before her tears were dry she found herself being ordered round as if she were a raw recruit under the command of a Sergeant-Major.

"Crying will do you no good," Mrs. Berkeley said sharply. "I have learnt in life that it is no use fighting the unchangeable—of which death is one."

She paused to say positively:

"Make up your mind once and for all that you are an extremely fortunate young woman in that I have taken you under my wing, and show your gratitude by trying to do what I require of you."

It would have been easier, Xenia thought, if there had been some method or routine in Mrs. Berkeley's requirements, but they changed not only day by day but hour by hour.

"But you told me to do that," she would sometimes expostulate when she was scolded and called a "nit-wit."

"Never mind what I said before," Mrs. Berkeley would snap, "this is what I want now, and I expect you to do it my way."

Sometimes Xenia had begun to wonder despairingly if perhaps she really was as stupid as Mrs. Berkeley told her she was.

Her father had always considered her intelligent, and her mother had loved her so deeply that it was almost impossible for her to find fault with such a beloved daughter.

It was after she had been with Mrs. Berkeley for nearly nine months that Xenia had come to the conclusion that a clue to Mrs. Berkeley's continual fault-finding where she was concerned was that she was too attractive.

It was impossible to alter the beauty that Xenia had inherited from her mother or conceal the fact that she looked different from other girls of her age.

People exclaimed at her appearance and paid her compliments which, she noticed, made Mrs. Berkeley's lips tighten in anger.

Her employer might now be well over forty, but she had been good-looking in her youth, and there was no doubt that she resented the way everyone who came to Berkeley Towers looked at Xenia in astonishment and kept on looking.

Sometimes Xenia would ask herself what was the point of having good looks if they were a hindrance rather than a help.

But there were moments when a glint of admiration in a man's eye, however old he might be, was a source of comfort.

'Perhaps one day,' she thought to herself, 'I shall meet somebody who will love me...then I shall escape.'

She knew it was wrong not to be more grateful to Mrs. Berkeley, but all day long she heard her voice calling her, berating her, criticising her, and sometimes jeering at her.

It was all so unlike the happiness she had known at home.

It had been very quiet in their small thatched cottage, which, however, had had many comforts compared to the other cottages in Little Coombe.

"Really, this place is almost habitable!" Mrs.

Berkeley had said when she came to the cottage after
the funeral.

She looked round at the attractive way in which
the small rooms were decorated and at the pieces
of good furniture which Xenia's father and mother
had collected over the years.

It was Mrs. Berkeley's condescension, Xenia
thought, that she resented more than anything else.

She often had to fight back an impulse to tell the
older woman the truth about her mother and watch
with amusement her change of attitude.

But that would have been betraying what Xenia
thought of as a sacred trust.

She was fourteen when Mrs. Sandon had said
one day:

"You must have wondered, my dearest, why I
have never talked to you about my father and mother, or my family."

Xenia had looked at her wide-eyed as she went
on:

"Your father's relatives all live in the North, although most of them are dead, but I have a family
too."

"You have, Mama?" Xenia exclaimed. "Why have
you never spoken of them to me?"

"Because my past is a secret and what I am going
to tell you must be a secret, Xenia. You must promise
me that you will never speak of it to anyone."

"Why not, Mama?"

"When your father and I ran away together to
make a new life of our own, I cut the links which
joined me not only to my father and mother but also
to my twin sister."

"Mama!"

Xenia's expression was one of sheer astonishment.

"You ran away with Papa?" she cried. "How exciting! How romantic!"

"It was," her mother said with a smile. "Very,
very romantic, and, Xenia, I have never regretted it.

It was not only the wisest thing I have ever done, but it also made me the happiest woman in the world!"

There was no doubt her father and mother were exceptionally happy.

Xenia had only to watch the expression on her mother's face when her father came into a room and see her father's eyes soften in adoration to know that they lived in a blissful world of their own.

"I have often wondered where you came from, Mama, but when I asked you you never told me, though I know it was somewhere in Europe."

"How did you know that?" Mrs. Sandon enquired.

Xenia laughed.

"People are always saying that your hair and mine are the colour of the Empress of Austria's, or else they say we must have Hungarian blood in our veins."

"Both are accurate," Mrs. Sandon said quietly.

"Then tell me . . . tell me everything, Mama, and I promise I will never reveal your secret to anyone."

Mrs. Sandon had paused for a moment, then she said:

"My father—your grandfather—is King Constantine of Slovia!"

Xenia stared at her open-mouthed.

"Is this true, Mama, or a fairy-story?"

"It is true," Mrs. Sandon said with a smile.

"Then why have you no title?"

"That is just what I am going to explain to you, dearest. I gave up everything when I ran away with your father."

Xenia clasped her hands together and listened intently as her mother with a far-away look in her eyes said:

"I wish you could have seen your father when he first came to the Palace. He was so handsome, so attractive in his uniform, and I felt my heart stop beating. I knew, I think, from that first moment I saw him that I was in love."

"And did he fall in love with you, Mama?" Xenia asked.

"Instantly!" Mrs. Sandon replied. "He told me afterwards that it was as if I was enveloped in a white light and I was what he had been searching for all his life and never found."

"And he told you that he felt like that?"

"Not at once," her mother answered. "It was difficult for us to be together, but somehow we managed it, and as we looked into each other's eyes and his hand touched mine there was no need for words: we knew we belonged to each other."

"What happened?" Xenia asked breathlessly.

"We fought against it. We both fought against something which we knew would cause not only consternation but unremitting anger."

"You mean that your father, the King, would not think Papa a suitable husband for you?" Xenia asked.

"He would not have imagined such an alliance to be within the realm of possibility," her mother replied. "It is doubtful if he even realised that your father existed."

"Why was he at your Palace?"

"He had come to Slovia as one of the Aides-de-Camp of an English General who was on a Military Mission."

"It must have been difficult for you ever to meet," Xenia said sympathetically.

"It would have been impossible if my twin sister had not looked exactly like me," her mother explained.

"You never told me that you had a twin sister," Xenia interrupted accusingly.

"If you only knew how much I longed to tell you about her and to talk about her," her mother answered. "I suppose it was inevitable, since twins are closer to each other than any other relations, that when I left home with your father, even though I loved him overwhelmingly one little part of me was left behind with Dorottyn."

"What a pretty name!" Xenia said. "I have always loved yours, Mama . . . Lilla."

7

"I wanted to change it to Lilly when I came to England," her mother answered, "but your father would not let me. He said Lilla suited me, and you know I always do what he wants."

"As he does what you want," Xenia said, laughing.

"I have been so very, very lucky," Mrs. Sandon said softly.

"You do not regret leaving a Palace and all your family behind?"

"I missed Dorottyn," her mother replied, "and I find it hard to forgive my father and mother for wiping me out of their lives and behaving as if I no longer exist."

"How could they do that?" Xenia asked indignantly.

"I suppose, looking back, my behaviour was outrageous from their point of view," Mrs. Sandon said. "I had not only fallen in love with a commoner, but had refused a very advantageous alliance they had arranged for me which they thought would benefit our country."

"I have always understood that Royal marriages were arranged," Xenia said.

"And a great many others as well," Mrs. Sandon agreed, "but Royal brides are supposed to have no feelings and no desires, and only a sense of duty to their country."

She laughed and threw out her arms.

"Oh, Xenia, how can I explain to you how different it is to be married to your father and to know I am loved for myself and nothing else. But I could bring him no dowry—nothing!"

"Did Papa have to leave the Regiment?"

"Of course," Mrs. Sandon said. "We had caused a scandal, and that was unforgivable. Everything was hushed up as much as possible, not only for my father's sake but because it was inconceivable that an English Aide-de-Camp should run away with a King's daughter! I believe it considerably upset the Military Mission."

Xenia laughed at the note in her mother's voice. "One would hardly think that mattered."

"There is very strict protocol in a Palace—everything matters!" Mrs. Sandon said. "So your father and I had to disappear."

"Is that why you came to Little Coombe?"

"Your father knew it, and when I saw the pretty village and the little house that was available for us it seemed to me my idea of Heaven," Mrs. Sandon said.

She looked at her daughter and went on:

"When you fall in love, my dearest, you will understand that all one wants is to be alone with the man you love and to look after him. Nothing else is of the least consequence."

"I am sure Papa thinks the same."

"He does, although he regrets, quite unnecessarily, that he cannot give me all the comforts I knew in Slovia."

"It is because you ran away that we have always been so poor?" Xenia asked.

"Exactly, my dearest. And although it has never worried me, I want so much for you that we cannot give you."

"I am very happy," Xenia said. "As long as I can ride with Papa and you can teach me so many things, I know I am lucky too."

Mrs. Sandon put her arm round Xenia and kissed her.

"That is exactly what I wanted you to say, my darling, when I told you my secret."

"It is a very exciting one!" Xenia exclaimed. "But why did your sister not keep in touch with you? She must have missed you too."

"I know Dorottyn missed me, just as I missed her," Mrs. Sandon agreed, "but she was left at home and there was no possibility of her communicating with me against our father's commands. In any case, she would not have known my address."

"You did not write?"

"No. I knew it would be an embarrassment."

"And has she married?"

"Yes. I saw the announcement of her marriage a year after I left Slovia, to the Arch-Duke Frederich of Prussen."

"That sounds very grand."

"He was in fact the man my father meant me to marry," her mother answered, "but I promise you, darling, that I have never for one moment wished to change places with my twin sister."

"Has she any children?" Xenia asked curiously.

"I do not know," Mrs. Sandon replied sadly. "You see, the English newspapers are not particularly interested in the smaller States of Europe. Sometimes there is a brief mention of Slovia, and two years ago I learnt that my mother was dead."

"Your father is still alive?"

"Yes. He is now an old man, and when I last read about him he was in ill health. I thought he might have come to England for one of the State occasions, but I imagine he was too ill to travel."

Xenia drew in her breath.

"It is hard to think of you, Mama, as the daughter of a King."

"It is something I had forgotten, and you too must forget," Mrs. Sandon said.

"I do not want to forget it," Xenia replied. "I want to remember it. Now I know why you have such dignity, Mama, and why Papa teases you about your aristocratic nose."

She jumped up to run to a mirror which hung on one wall of the room.

"I have a nose like yours," she said. "In fact I look very much like you, with my red hair and green eyes. Do you think I look aristocratic?"

"I hope you will always behave as if you are," Mrs. Sandon said, "and that means being both proud and brave, and considerate and understanding of other people."

"Just like you," Xenia said. "I will try, Mama. I will, really! It is all very exciting!"

"Not really," Mrs. Sandon replied. "And remember, Xenia, you can never tell anyone who I am. My father, as did my mother when she was alive, behaves as if I were dead."

There was a little throb in her mother's voice which was very moving and Xenia ran to put her arms round her neck.

"Never mind, Mama," she said. "You have Papa and me and we love you very, very much."

"That is all that matters," Mrs. Sandon said. "And I promise you, Xenia, that it is far better to be in a house of love than in the grandest Palace in the whole world."

Xenia thought that her mother had spoken very truly when she found in the huge luxury of Berkeley Towers no love and very little consideration for other people.

"Good gracious, girl, but you have been a long time!" Mrs. Berkeley had remarked disagreeably when she brought her something she had requested but which had been difficult to find.

"It was right at the top of the house," Xenia explained apologetically.

"I am sure you can run up a few stairs at your age!" Mrs. Berkeley had retorted. "When I want something, I want it at once! You must make up your mind to hurry."

"I have hurried," Xenia wanted to say.

It was no use arguing, she thought, for Mrs. Berkeley would find fault whatever she did.

On other occasions she had rebuked Xenia for running up and down the stairs, saying that it was undignified and a bad example to the servants.

At night when she lay in the large, comfortable bed-room with which she was provided at Berkeley Towers because it was near to her mistress and she could be summoned at a moment's notice, she longed

11

for the tiny bed-room with its sloping ceiling she had occupied at home.

There, with its little casement of diamond panes under the thatch, she had thought the world outside was full of sunshine and laughter.

Inside the tiny cottage there had been an atmosphere of peace and contentment that she had not really appreciated until it was lost.

"You are not listening to what I am saying, Xenia!" Mrs. Berkeley said snappily now.

"I am sorry," Xenia said quickly. "The wheels are so noisy."

"I do not expect to have to say the same thing twice to anyone. I was telling you that you must be very careful with our hand-baggage when we reach Dover. All Continentals are thieves and robbers, and I do not wish to find my precious possessions have all disappeared while you are wool-gathering."

"I will be very careful," Xenia promised.

"So I should hope," Mrs. Berkeley said. "After all, it has cost me a lot of money to bring you on this trip."

"I know that," Xenia said, "and I have thanked you many, many times."

"As you should!" Mrs. Berkeley replied. "That gown alone cost a considerable sum. After all, I can hardly have a companion travelling with me looking like a ragged beggar."

This was untrue and offensive and Xenia felt the colour come into her cheeks, but she had learnt by now to say nothing to such taunts.

Mrs. Berkeley had gone out of her way to disparage the clothes she was wearing when she took her from the cottage to Berkeley Towers.

They were, it was true, of cheap materials, but they had been beautifully made by her mother and were in perfect taste.

Mrs. Berkeley had bought Xenia some black gowns, but after she had been in mourning for only five months she had suddenly commanded her to dispense with everything she owned that was black.

"I dislike the colour," she said. "Besides, it makes you look far too theatrical with that anaemic white skin of yours and that ostentatious red hair."

Obediently Xenia had put on the gowns she had worn before her father and mother died, only to be ridiculed and feel obliged to be effusively grateful for the gowns which Mrs. Berkeley bought her in their place.

She was well aware that they also annoyed her employer because every colour seemed to accentuate the whiteness of her skin.

"She has a skin like yours, darling," she had heard her father say once to her mother. "It is like a magnolia both to touch and to kiss."

Mrs. Berkeley's choice of gowns kept most of Xenia's magnolia-like skin well concealed, but there was nothing she could do about her hair.

It was the Titian red beloved by artists and was exactly the same colour as Winterhalter had portrayed in his picture of Elizabeth, Empress of Austria.

"Are we related to the most beautiful Queen in Europe?" Xenia had asked her mother once.

"As a matter of fact she is a distant cousin," her mother replied, "and there is also Hungarian blood in you."

She smiled as she went on:

"Now you understand why I want you to learn both German and Hungarian. Your father thought it was unnecessary, but I insisted."

"Perhaps one day, Mama, I could go to Slovia."

"Our people are a mixture of both the nations on either side of us," her mother explained. "But we have fused the languages together, and while a lot of words are German, others are completely Hungarian."

There had been an expression on her face which told Xenia she was looking back into the past as she said:

"My father had always insisted we should be good

13

linguists and be able to talk to our neighbours in their own language. I remember when the King of Luthenia visited us he was delighted because both Dorottyn and I could talk to him in Luthenian."

"I feel I shall never be as proficient as you, Mama."

"It is difficult to learn a language if you have never visited the country of its origin," Mrs. Sandon said, "but you will find when you do that it is not difficult if you know German, French, and Hungarian, and perhaps a little Greek, to speak all the Balkan languages."

After Xenia had learnt her mother's secret she studied assiduously the languages which previously she had thought, as had her father, were rather a waste of time.

When she and Mrs. Sandon were alone together they never spoke English.

Soon Xenia began to dream that one day, even if she went in the cheapest possible manner, she would visit Slovia and the other Kingdoms which her mother had known so well.

Now, she thought, it was one step forward that Mrs. Berkeley was taking her to France.

"I do not suppose you know any French," her employer remarked.

She spoke in a manner that made Xenia feel that she hoped she was right and would therefore be able to show her own superiority.

"I speak French," Xenia answered.

"You do?" Mrs. Berkeley raised her eye-brows, then added: "But of course you have foreign blood in you. There is no doubt of that. Neither you nor your late mother looked English."

It was not a compliment and Xenia could not help replying:

"Mama was not English! She came from the Balkans."

"Oh—the Balkans!" Mrs. Berkeley made it sound

as if there was something degrading about such a connection.

Because Xenia was afraid she might lose her temper she had quickly changed the subject.

Now she wondered if her mother would be pleased that she was going to France.

Often when she was alone in bed she would talk to her mother just as if she were there, telling her how miserable she was without her.

At the same time, she knew it would be the utmost selfishness on her part to wish either her father or her mother to be alive without the other.

They had loved her, she did not doubt that, but their real love had been for each other and she knew that if either of them had survived they would have wanted only to die so that they could be together.

Mrs. Berkeley looked at her watch.

"We should not be long now," she said. "Really, I find travelling by train extremely tiring. I am sure the poor creatures in the Second and Third-Class carriages find it quite exhausting."

This remark, Xenia knew, was intended to point out to her how fortunate she was to be able to travel in expensive luxury.

The words were just about to come obediently to her lips when suddenly there was a noise like an explosion and at the same time a crash which made the whole coach shudder. There was a shrill scream from Mrs. Berkeley and the coach turned over.

Xenia did not scream, she only knew a fear that made her reach out with her hands to hold on to something and find it was not there.

Then she was hurled sideways and lost consciousness. . . .

* * *

Xenia came slowly back to reality to hear a noise that was almost indescribable beating in her ears, and she became aware that she was lying on the ground.

She was vaguely aware that somebody lifted her, carried her a little way, and put her down on the grass.

Without opening her eyes, she heard shouts and screams mingled with the shrill hiss of escaping steam, which made all other sounds indistinguishable.

Then she felt herself being picked up again and because she was dazed and still only half-conscious she did not make any effort to show that she was aware of what was happening.

It slowly percolated into her mind that she was on a stretcher of some sort, but the noise made it hard to think.

The sound of escaping steam seemed to intensify so that after a moment she thought that whoever carried her must be taking her past the engine.

They went on, then a man's voice said:

"It's a relief we found her so quickly! That's a bit of luck, and better still that the station's so near."

"I know what has ... happened," Xenia told herself. "I have been in a ... railway crash."

It seemed to her silly that she had not realised it before, but it had all occurred so quickly, the shaking coach, the explosion, then unconsciousness.

Vaguely she told herself that she should ask about Mrs. Berkeley, but it was too much effort.

She felt herself drifting away into oblivion ... until once again she became aware of what was happening and realised that she was being carried into a building, for she could hear heavy footsteps on wooden boards.

"She'll be all right here," a man's voice said. "I'll send along a doctor if I can get hold of one."

"You'd better do that," another man replied, "and tell his Nibs we've got 'old of her. Ravin' like a madman, he was!"

Xenia felt herself put down on the floor. There

16

was the sound of two men leaving the room and shutting the door behind them.

She lay still for some minutes, then with an effort opened her eyes.

She found herself looking at a ceiling, at walls painted an unpleasant shade of brown, and guessed she was in a Waiting-Room of a station.

Hazily she remembered someone saying that the station was near to the scene of the accident.

She forced herself to sit up and found she was right in thinking she had been carried on a stretcher. It had been put down on a linoleum-covered floor.

The room was smaller than the usual Waiting-Room and besides the inevitable hard bench there were two arm-chairs in front of a fireplace.

Slowly, very, very slowly, Xenia rose to her feet. 'There are no bones broken,' she thought with satisfaction.

Indeed, apart from the fact that she had a headache, there was really nothing wrong.

However, feeling weak and rather frightened, she sat down on the bench.

Her hands were bare, her gloves were lost . . . she undid the ribbons of her bonnet and drew it from her head, feeling she would be able to think more clearly without it.

"There has . . . been a . . . railway accident," she told herself. "The train must have hit something, perhaps another . . . train, and the . . . collision forced it . . . off the . . . line."

She gave a sigh and found that she was shaking and her hands as well as her legs felt unsteady.

'That is . . . shock,' she thought practically. 'What I . . . ought to . . . have now is a . . . warm drink.'

Then hurriedly, because she was ashamed of thinking so much about herself, she decided she must find out what had happened to Mrs. Berkeley.

It seemed strange that more people were not being brought into the Waiting-Room.

She noticed that there were two doors and the one at the far end of the room had opaque glass panels and looked as if it might lead into a cloak-room.

Once again Xenia got to her feet.

Her hip felt a little bruised, but there was obviously nothing wrong with any other part of her body. She walked to the door and opened it.

She had been right. It was a cloak-room and over the basin there was a looking-glass.

She stared at herself, seeing that her face was very pale with shock, which made her eyes seem dark and enormous.

"I will have a ... drink of ... water," she decided, "then I will go in ... search of ... Mrs. Berkeley."

There were two glasses on the basin and she let the tap run, as her mother had always taught her to do to remove any rust or dirt that might have accumulated in it, and filled one of the glasses.

The water was cold and it seemed to clear away some of her feelings of shock and inertia.

'I really must ... try to find ... Mrs. Berkeley,' she thought.

She washed her hands with cold water, then pressed them against her forehead.

"I have to ... think clearly. I am unhurt ... and I must ... find Mrs. Berkeley."

She felt as if the words repeated and rerepeated themselves in her mind, then resolutely she turned back towards the Waiting-Room.

As she opened the door she saw that while she had been away, someone else had come into the room.

It was a woman and she had her back to Xenia as she walked towards the bench on which she had left her bonnet.

She had reached it and picked it up by its ribbons when the woman turned round.

For a moment Xenia thought it was hard to see

18

her properly. She told herself that her eyes were out of focus and that she was still looking at her reflection in the mirror in the cloak-room.

'I am ... still dazed,' she thought.

Then the woman spoke.

"Good heavens!" she exclaimed. "Who are you?"

Xenia found it impossible to reply.

As she stared at the stranger she saw that she had the same red hair, the same white skin, and the same green eyes framed with dark lashes as she had.

"What is your name?"

The question was sharp and had an authoritative note in it.

"X-Xenia ... Sandon."

"I might have guessed it without having to ask you."

"Y-you ... mean ... ?"

"You are my cousin. I always knew I had one, but I did not expect her to look so exactly like me, even though our mothers were twins."

The information burst into Xenia's bemused consciousness like the explosion of a fire-bomb.

"Y-you mean ... you are the daughter of ... my Aunt ... Dorottyn?"

"Of course! My name is Johanna—or rather Johanna Xenia. I believe our mothers promised each other that if they had a daughter she would be called Xenia, which was the name of their favourite doll."

Xenia laughed. It was a shaky little sound.

"Mama told me that ... but I never believed ... I never thought ... there would be anyone in the whole world who looked ... so like me."

"We are exactly alike," Johanna said. "But it is not really surprising, considering that our mothers looked identical, and I look exactly like mine."

"As I look ... like mine," Xenia replied.

She swayed a little as she spoke and Johanna said:

"You had better sit down. Were you hurt?"

19

"No. I was only knocked ... unconscious for a moment and they carried me in ... here."

Johanna gave a little laugh.

"Do you know," she said, "I think they thought they were carrying me."

"Why do you say that?" Xenia asked.

She looked up at her cousin in a puzzled manner.

"Well, this happens to be the special station of the Lord Warden of the Cinque Ports—at least so I was told—and I imagine this is the private room reserved only for him. The rest of the passengers will be in the public Waiting-Rooms."

"Oh ... I see ..." Xenia said. "I remember now that a man said: 'It's a relief we found her so soon.'"

"Then they did think that you were me," Johanna answered.

She sat down in a chair beside Xenia and there was a silence before she asked:

"Where are you going? Why were you on the train?"

"I am going to France with a Mrs. Berkeley, to whom I am ... a companion. My father and mother both ... died last ... year."

"I am sorry," Johanna said. "That must have been terrible for you."

"We were very happy," Xenia answered.

Her cousin looked at her searchingly.

"Do you mean that? Was your mother really happy after she ran away? I have often wondered, and I know my mother wondered too."

"Mama and Papa were blissfully happy together," Xenia replied. "Mama often said that she never regretted having to be poor with Papa in a tiny cottage instead of living in a Palace."

"Your mother was exceptional. I do not believe I should ever feel like that."

"You would, if you were in love."

"I am in love," Johanna said, "but how can I give

20

up everything—everything I have always known—even to be with Robert?"

Xenia looked at her in surprise.

"Are you in love with an Englishman?"

"Yes, just like your mother, with an Englishman."

"And are you going to run away with him?"

"I would like to," Johanna replied, "but quite frankly, I am not brave enough."

"Then you are not really in love."

"It is all very well for you to talk like that, but I am to marry King István of Luthenia, so I should not only have my father and mother furious with me, but him as well."

"Mama was in exactly the same position," Xenia said. "She was supposed to marry the Arch-Duke Frederi..."

She stopped suddenly, remembering her mother had told her that he had afterwards married her twin sister.

Johanna was staring at her incredulously.

"Do you really mean that your mother was supposed to marry my Papa?"

She threw back her head and laughed.

"Oh, now I understand so many things that were kept from me! It must have infuriated Papa to think that anybody could turn him down for a commoner, and an Englishman at that!"

"But he married your mother," Xenia said quickly.

"I suppose in his eyes one twin was as good as another," Johanna admitted. "But I am not surprised that your mother's name is taboo. I can only talk about her when I am alone with Mama."

"My mother never knew of your existence," Xenia said. "She longed to know if Aunt Dorottyn had any children, but there was no way for her to find out and there seemed to be very little news about Slovia in the English newspapers."

"There is very little about England in ours," Johanna replied, as if wishing to sound patriotic, "except that we all have to kow-tow to your Queen, and goodness knows she is a frightening person!"

"You have seen her?" Xenia asked.

"I have been staying for two nights at Windsor Castle, which is one of the reasons why I was allowed to come to England. Robert was there and it was very wonderful when we could snatch a few moments together."

Her face seemed suddenly illuminated for a moment. Then she said:

"But it is no use. I have been sent for urgently and told that it is imperative that I should go to Luthenia at once. There is nothing I can do but obey."

There was a note of despondency in her voice, then suddenly she stared at Xenia and said:

"Listen—I have an idea!"

"An idea?" Xenia questioned.

"Quickly follow what I have to say, for we have very little time."

"What do you . . . mean? What are you . . . talking about?"

Johanna glanced over her shoulder as if she thought someone might be listening. Then she said:

"I had planned—never mind how, because it was very difficult—I had planned to spend ten days with Robert before I returned home. He had everything arranged and we were going to be together for the last time in our lives."

There was a sob in Johanna's voice as she went on:

"Then I had this summons to go immediately to Luthenia, and the British Foreign Office with our Embassy has made all the arrangements."

She paused before she said:

"But now that I have found you, I can be with Robert after all, and no-one will ever know that I am not in Luthenia."

"Wh-what . . . are you saying?" Xenia asked.

"You said you are only the companion to some woman. If you just disappear, would she worry unduly about you?"

"I expect she would make ... enquiries. ..."

"She would think you were killed, crushed or something by the train," Johanna said. "But what you would really be doing is travelling to Luthenia instead of me!"

"You are crazy! How could I do such a thing?" Xenia asked.

"Who is to know, looking as you do?" Johanna enquired.

She jumped to her feet.

"Listen, Xenia, someone may come in at any moment and by that time we have to change our clothes."

"I ... I cannot do it ... they would find ... me out."

"No they will not," Johanna contradicted. "If you do not know everything you are expected to know, just say you are dazed and have lost your memory. It would be quite understandable in the circumstances."

Xenia stared at her wide-eyed.

"Are you really suggesting ... I should ... impersonate you?"

"Listen to me," Johanna said. "All you have to do is to travel to Luthenia and find out why they are in such a flutter. My engagement was announced three months ago, but we are not to be married until the autumn. I suppose there is some ceremony or other at which I am expected to appear, but it will not be of any consequence."

"But ... the K-King ... your ... f-fiancé, will know I am not ... you."

"He is not likely to pay you very much attention, judging from his behaviour in the past," Johanna said scathingly.

"Why not? I do not understand."

"I will tell you while we change. Come on—come

quickly into the cloak-room—you must put on my dress and I will put on yours."

"We cannot ... I mean ... it is impossible!" Xenia tried to say.

But Johanna had taken her by the hand and was pulling her across the small room, with her other hand picking up her bonnet as she went.

Inside the cloak-room, she locked the door and said:

"Now, start taking off your clothes."

"You are mad!" Xenia protested. "The minute I open my mouth people will realise something strange has happened."

"Nobody in Luthenia has ever heard of you," Johanna said. "You speak Slovian."

It was a statement more than a question.

"Yes, of course!" Xenia answered. "Mama taught me all the languages she spoke. As it happens, Luthenian is almost the same as Slovian."

"Then what are you fussing about?" Johanna asked. "What you have to do is to smile at everything they say and make yourself pleasant. Then I will join you and you can go back to England."

She paused, then said:

"I will pay you, of course. I will pay you for doing this. Now let me think—in English currency I will give you one hundred ... no, two hundred pounds."

"Two hundred pounds?" Xenia gasped.

It was more than she could earn from Mrs. Berkeley in years.

"I can get hold of two hundred without there being any questions asked," Johanna said, "and besides that, if you are in real trouble, Robert—Lord Gratton is his name—will help you. He will be so grateful that we can spend our time together as we planned."

"How did you meet him?" Xenia asked, because she was curious.

Johanna smiled. It was an uncanny sight to Xenia

because it was almost like seeing her own lips smile.

"Robert was sent out to the British Embassy in Slovia. We met and fell head-over-heels in love with each other, and that was that!"

"But you will not run away with him?"

"He wanted me to, and he is quite prepared to give up his diplomatic career. But how can I refuse to be a Queen? Besides, I think Papa would almost kill me!"

"Mama never regretted running away with the man she loved."

"I will settle for the moment for having ten days with Robert, as we promised ourselves," Johanna said, and added:

"Come on, Xenia. Do hurry and get changed. They are certain to find my tiresome ladies-in-waiting at any moment."

"You cannot . . . do this to me . . . you cannot . . . Johanna," Xenia protested. "What ladies-in-waiting, and what will they think?"

"They will think nothing," Johanna said rather too quickly for it to sound convincing. "The only danger is the Baroness von Absicht, who came with me from Slovia. She is a rather nosy old thing. At the same time, how could she imagine for one single moment that you and I would meet for the first time owing to a train crash?"

"It does sound very far-fetched," Xenia agreed.

"It is like a plot in one of the lurid novelettes Mama will not let me read," Johanna said. "But I must tell you about the rest of my party."

"I . . . I cannot do it!"

"You have to help me, Xenia," Johanna pleaded. "Besides, you need two hundred pounds—you know you do!"

That was irrefutably true, and, taking off her gown, Xenia listened as Johanna went on:

"The other lady-in-waiting, Madame Gyula, comes from Luthenia and only joined me today in London, so she is no menace; but, there is my lady's-maid."

"She will certainly be suspicious."

"She will only think that I am rather dazed, and suffering perhaps from brain damage, after the train crash," Johanna said positively. "We had better change our underclothes as well. Yours look somewhat inferior to mine. I am not meaning to be rude."

"I have never seen anything so beautiful as yours," Xenia replied.

"Well, you can have the use of them and all the clothes I have with me. They are quite attractive, because they are to be part of my trousseau. I picked a number of them up in Paris on my way to England."

"You are quite sure you do not mind me wearing them?"

"You will have nothing else to wear," Johanna said. "The one thing you cannot do is claim your own luggage."

Xenia clasped her hands together.

"Oh, Johanna, do not make me do this! I shall be so frightened ... so terrified of making a mistake. After all, I have never lived in a Palace."

"You need not worry about that," Johanna said. "There is always some interfering old woman to tell you what to do: 'Do not forget your gloves, Your Royal Highness'; 'You must curtsey, Your Royal Highness'; 'Shake hands with the Mayor, Your Royal Highness.' Sometimes I could scream!"

"I will be grateful for any help I can find," Xenia said.

Johanna smiled.

"I know you will not let me down, and just think how happy I shall be with Robert! We are going to a small house he owns in Cornwall. We shall be completely alone there."

Xenia looked at her wide-eyed.

"Completely alone ... Do you mean ...? Are you telling me ...?"

"That Robert is my lover? Of course he is! And has been for over a year!"

26

"Oh, Johanna . . . I never imagined . . . I never knew that . . . anyone . . ."

"Could behave in such an outrageous way?" Johanna finished. "I cannot think where you have been brought up, Xenia, but it does happen continually in every country in the world."

She was laughing at her, Xenia knew. At the same time, she was shocked.

She had never imagined that a girl of her own age who belonged to a decent family could actually have a lover when she was engaged to another man.

"B-but the King?" she stammered after a moment.

"The King has Elga—a mistress with whom he is infatuated—and we have already agreed that once we are married we will lead our private lives in our own way."

Xenia did not answer and Johanna said:

"That shocks you too."

"It does rather," Xenia admitted. "It seems such a cold-blooded, unpleasant way of being married."

"It is unpleasant to have to marry a man you do not love," Johanna snapped. "Even living the life of a commoner as you have, you must be aware that Royalty have certain obligations which they cannot ignore."

"Mama ignored them."

"And shocked the whole of Europe! Oh, I know it was supposed to be kept quiet," Johanna said, "but of course it was whispered from Court to Court. They not only thought your mother was crazy to make such a choice, they thought it was a blow at the Monarchy."

"Mama never thought she was so important," Xenia said.

"Well, she was, and I do not want to be held up as a terrible example," Johanna said.

Then as she looked at her cousin's troubled eyes she bent forward and kissed her.

"Stop worrying about me, Xenia. I am doing what

27

is right—for me, at any rate. I can never thank you enough for helping to make Robert and me happy for ten days."

She paused to say solemnly:

"It will be all I will have to remember in the years to come."

"Change your mind and marry him," Xenia pleaded.

"No!" Johanna replied. "I am engaged to King István and I intend to be a Queen. All you have to do is keep the place warm for me so that there will be no scandal."

"But how will we join each other?"

"Leave all that to me," Johanna said. "I will turn up at the Palace somehow, and then all you will have to do is take your money and come home."

It all sounded very easy, but Xenia thought she must still be suffering from shock and was too dazed to go on protesting.

"What about you?" she asked rather feebly. "How will you find ... what was his name ... Lord Gratton ... again?"

"Fate moves in a mysterious way," Johanna answered. "Robert intends, although I warned him it would be dangerous, to meet me in Dover. He went by an earlier train, and he was somehow going to arrange for us to say good-bye before I boarded the cross-Channel Steamer."

She was buttoning Xenia's blue gown as she went on:

"It is arranged that we shall go to the Lord Warden Hotel on arrival. Robert will be there, and when I tell him that I am free to go away with him I know how grateful he will be to you, as I am."

"He will be upset if he learns you have been in a railway accident," Xenia said.

"I imagine that they will get the passengers who are not hurt to Dover as quickly as possible," Johanna replied. "Anyway, do not worry about me. I have plenty of money and I can look after myself."

"I think you are very brave."

"I think you are an angel, and that is what really matters."

"On the contrary, I must be a little soft in the head—otherwise I would never agree to this wild scheme!"

"It is foolproof. What are you fussing about?" Johanna asked. "Look at us. Who could think in a thousand years there could be two cousins who look exactly alike? It was so long ago that everybody has forgotten that your mother and mine were identical twins."

"Your mother!" Xenia exclaimed. "Supposing she sees me?"

"She will not," Johanna replied confidently. "And even if she and Papa wished to turn up in Luthenia because I was there, it would be impossible for them to do so within the next ten days."

"Why is that?"

"Because they are the guests of the Tsar in Saint Petersburg and they cannot get back from Russia in a hurry."

"No, that is true," Xenia said with a sigh of relief.

"Now do not worry!" Johanna admonished. "All you have to do is be limp and let everybody take care of you. They are very good at that. It drives me insane! But then, as my mother often says, I have Papa's bossiness and his inclination to give rather than take orders."

"Your father would be . . . horrified if he knew what we were . . . doing," Xenia said.

"He will never know," Johanna replied confidently. "By the way, Papa, Mama, and King István call me Xenia, but no-one else does."

"How strange! Why do they do that?"

"Mama wanted it to be my only name, because she had promised your mother to call her daughter Xenia. But Papa insisted on my being called after his grandmother, while King István says that Johanna was the name of an aunt he hated!"

Xenia laughed before she said:

"Well, at least I shall answer when he speaks to me."

Johanna looked at herself in the mirror.

Xenia's gown of deep blue with its tight bodice showed her small waist above the full skirt draped over her hips.

"This gown is not too bad," she said. "I might look worse."

"But you have nothing else to wear."

"That is of no consequence," Johanna answered. "Robert can buy me everything I need in Dover, and actually I shall want very little—except his arms about me!"

She spoke in a way which made Xenia blush. Then before she could say anything more there was a knock on the door.

"Are you all right, Your Royal Highness?" a man's voice asked.

"Quite all right, thank you, Mr. Donington," Johanna replied. "I am just tidying myself. I shall be out in a moment."

"There is no hurry, Your Royal Highness."

"Thank you."

They heard footsteps move away from the door.

"Who was that?" Xenia asked in a whisper.

"Mr. Somerset Donington," Johanna explained against her cousin's ear. "He is from the British Foreign Office."

"Will he be suspicious?"

"No. He has never seen me before today."

Xenia gave a little sigh of relief.

"Now go into the room," Johanna ordered. "Just be vague and appear to be suffering from shock."

"And you?"

"I shall wait here until you are out of the way."

"I . . . I cannot . . . do it!"

Johanna only kissed her swiftly again on the cheek and without saying anything opened the door.

She stood behind it and there was nothing Xenia could do but walk forward into the Waiting-Room.

There was a middle-aged man with a worried expression on his face waiting for her.

"I am sorry I have been so long, Your Royal Highness," he said, "but I have some rather bad news for you."

It was impossible for Xenia to trust her voice. She could only look at him questioningly.

"I am afraid both the Baroness von Absicht and your lady's-maid are too badly injured to continue the journey. They have been taken by ambulance to a Hospital in Dover, where the doctors think they will have to remain for at least two or three weeks."

"I am very sorry to hear that."

Xenia was surprised that she could speak clearly and did not stammer, and she thought that Johanna would be proud of her.

"I have, however, found Madame Gyula," Mr. Donington continued. "She is only a little shaken, and is waiting for Your Royal Highness now in a carriage outside."

"We are to travel by carriage?" Xenia asked.

"It is only about three-quarters of an hour's drive to Dover," Mr. Donington answered, "and I thought, Ma'am, you would find it less irksome to get away at once rather than wait for another train."

"Of course," Xenia agreed.

"Then shall we go?"

"Y-yes..."

She walked across the room, wondering as she did so if Johanna thought she was doing her part well.

'This is mad! Crazy! It will end up in a lot of trouble!' she thought to herself.

Then she thought that whatever happened, it was infinitely preferable to being nagged at and found fault with by Mrs. Berkeley.

What was more, it was an adventure—a wild, exciting adventure—when she had least expected it!

31

Chapter Two

Nearing Vienna, Xenia suddenly felt panic-stricken at what lay ahead.

Up till now everything had gone smoothly, but a hundred times a day she thought the people with her must realise she was not who she pretended to be.

They accepted the fact that she was upset, dazed, and a little absent-minded after the train accident.

From the moment she crossed the Channel in a private cabin with two plain-clothes policemen to guard her she knew that the die was cast and there was no going back.

It was perhaps fortunate that Madame Gyula was in a worse state than was Xenia herself. A woman of over forty, she had been not only shocked but considerably frightened by the collision.

Over and over again she bemoaned the fact that she had ever been persuaded to escort the Princess to Luthenia.

"The King should have sent someone younger," she wailed, "but of course His Majesty trusts me, and what will he say when he hears what has happened to Your Royal Highness!"

"He can hardly blame you for the railway crash," Xenia felt obliged to say comfortingly.

"King István is very organised, as you know,

Your Royal Highness. He expects everyone to obey his orders implicitly."

She had referred several times to the King's love of order, which made Xenia feel that he might be as pompous and authoritative as was Johanna's father.

Her mother had told her that the Arch-Duke Frederich was an autocrat and something of a tyrant.

"I should have been so unhappy with him," she had said. "I like people who are warm and loving, like your Papa, although sometimes I wish he was a little more practical where money matters are concerned."

It had been a shock to Xenia to discover that when her father and mother died not only were they in debt but how very little money they had actually had to live on all the years they had been at Little Coombe.

Her father had come from an Army family, and her grandfather, Major General Sir Alexander Sandon, had written her a stiff letter on her father's death which told her he had never really forgiven his son for having left his Regiment.

The General's letter to Xenia was sharply to the point:

It is impossible for me to come South to attend your father's Funeral, and his two brothers are with the Regiment in India. You are of course aware that your father has received an allowance from me for the last nineteen years. As I imagine you have not been left well off, I will continue to send you half the amount I gave my son, which will be paid to you quarterly through my Solicitors.

There had been no intimation in the letter that he wished to see Xenia, and although she was not particularly surprised, it was hurtful to think he still resented the fact that her mother had spoilt his son's Army career.

The allowance Xenia was to receive was, she found, a little under one hundred pounds a year, which meant that her father and mother had received two hundred pounds.

It was enough to keep them from starvation, but Xenia understood now why so many economies had to be made even to live as quietly as they had in Little Coombe.

She thought there might have been some money left for her after the sale of the cottage, which she knew had been bought with the jewellery which her mother had brought with her when she ran away from Slovia.

But the cottage was mortgaged, and by the time that had been paid off and Xenia had reluctantly sold the furniture, she had so little in the Bank that she was afraid for the future.

"I shall have to find some sort of employment," she told herself, and when Mrs. Berkeley suggested she should come to her as a companion, she knew that she had no alternative.

'Whatever happens in the future,' she thought now, 'I shall have two hundred pounds from Johanna and memories that I would never have had otherwise.'

At the same time, she was frightened.

It was one thing to convince herself that she was so like Johanna that nobody could possibly suspect she was anyone else, but she knew it depended largely on the fact that she was surrounded by people who did not know her cousin well.

Mr. Somerset Donington, like Madame Gyula, had met Johanna only the day before they had left London. But Xenia had learnt that when they reached Vienna she was to be handed over to the care of a Luthenian Statesman, as they would then travel in the King's private train.

It had been exciting to find that there was a whole coach engaged for her on the train from Calais to Paris.

Xenia had longed to ask if it was possible for her to see the city of which she had heard so much, and it was disappointing to find that there was only just time to catch the night-train, which would travel right across Europe and from which she would disembark at Vienna.

Mr. Donington kept apologising for the fact that she had no lady's-maid.

"I am sure Madame Gyula will help you, Ma'am, where she can," he said. "There was no time for me to engage a woman, but I have sent a telegram to His Majesty to explain what has happened and ask if one could be in attendance on the Royal Train."

"I am sure that His Majesty will not wish to be bothered with such a small detail," Xenia said.

"I know that everything which concerns Your Royal Highness's comfort is to him of the greatest importance," Mr. Donington replied diplomatically.

Xenia hoped that when she was alone with Madame Gyula she would be able to find out some intimate details about the King which would be a guide and help when she actually met him.

But Madame Gyula could only moan about herself and the accident and be quite certain that the King would hold her personally responsible for what had happened.

'If he frightens old women like Madame,' Xenia thought to herself, 'he will certainly frighten me!'

When she was lying in bed that night in the coach which had been reserved for her and which she knew was guarded all the time by plain-clothes policemen, she continually told herself that this was an exciting adventure which she would always remember.

She felt that in a way her mother would help her and protect her from making any serious mistakes; and what was more important than anything else was that she should not let Johanna down.

Whatever her cousin had said about the King having love-affairs of his own, she was quite certain he

would not expect his future wife and Queen to have a
lover.

Xenia blushed at the very word.

How could any well-bred girl, and her mother's
niece in particular, go away with a man as if she were
married to him?

Xenia was very innocent and had no idea exactly what happened when a man and a woman made
love to each other.

But she had only to think of her mother and father
to know that it was something very intimate and
what they did was also blessed by God.

To make love with a man for ten days, intending
never afterwards to see him again, struck her as
wrong, if not wicked.

"How can she behave like that?" she asked herself. "To do so she must love him, but not enough to
give up the chance of being a Queen."

She thought that if she fell in love she would
behave in exactly the same way as her mother had
done and nothing and nobody should stand in her
way.

And if she was half as happy as her father and
mother had been, then everything, however contro-
versial, would be worthwhile.

Nevertheless, at the moment it was impossible not
to enjoy being made a fuss of and deferred to with
respect, which was certainly a change from Mrs.
Berkeley's incessant fault-finding.

Mr. Somerset Donington was a Diplomat of the
old type, who said all the charming things a Royal
person wished to hear and who smoothed over every
difficulty with an expertise which came from long years
of practice.

It was just before they neared Vienna that Xenia
asked him:

"Do tell me, Mr. Donington, why have I been
summoned from England so hurriedly to Luthenia?"

She saw that Mr. Donington looked embarrassed.

He did not answer at once and she said:

"It would be kind of you to tell me the truth. I do not wish to make any mistakes when I arrive in Molnár."

This was the Capital of Luthenia, where they were to meet the King.

"No, of course not," Mr. Donington agreed, "but I am sure Your Royal Highness will have a very warm welcome from the Luthenians, and they will be greatly looking forward to your marriage."

Xenia did not answer and he went on:

"I understand, Ma'am, that you have not visited your future country since your engagement was announced?"

"No," Xenia said.

"Then you may expect many demonstrations of enthusiasm," Mr. Donington said. "I am sure you are aware, Your Royal Highness, that the Luthenians are a warm, extroverted people, who at times get carried away."

"What do you mean by that?" Xenia asked.

She thought that Mr. Donington wished he had phrased his statement differently, but he replied:

"The Luthenians are noted as being somewhat temperamental, which of course owes more to their Hungarian blood than their Austrian."

"I have always heard," Xenia said, "that the Austrian Court under the Hapsburgs is very stiff and the protocol extremely rigid compared to anywhere else."

This was something she had heard from her mother, and Mr. Donington agreed, saying:

"That is true, but, as you know, King István is very different from the Emperor Franz Josef."

"Tell me how you see him, Mr. Donington."

"I would hardly presume, Your Royal Highness . . ." Mr. Donington began, but Xenia said earnestly:

"I would like to know the truth. I want to help my future country and it will be easier for me to do so if I know how the King is thought of by Diplomats like yourself in England and in other parts of Europe."

She thought Mr. Donington looked surprised. At the same time, he was impressed by her sincerity.

"Luthenia," he said after a moment's thought, "is a very important country at the moment in the balance of power. Your father will doubtless have told you that there is always the fear of the Ottoman Empire expanding further Northwards, and the Austrian Empire has ambitions of expanding Southwards."

Xenia realised she was expected to reply, and she said:

"Yes, I understood that."

"I am sure Her Majesty Queen Victoria told you the same thing," Mr. Donington said with a smile. "I suspect it was one of the reasons why Your Royal Highness was invited to Windsor Castle."

Rather than lie, Xenia gave him a little smile and he continued:

"King István is therefore in an ideal position to become extremely important, with the support and blessing of Great Britain, France, and Germany."

Mr. Donington paused, then added:

"I have met His Majesty only once, but he struck me as being an exceptionally gifted young man, which would be greatly enhanced if he were to dedicate himself to the cause of Luthenia."

"Do you think he does not do that already?" Xenia asked.

Now Mr. Donington looked extremely embarrassed.

"I assure Your Royal Highness that I was not criticising His Majesty in any way."

"No, of course not," Xenia said, "but I am anxious to know exactly what the King could do."

Mr. Donington leant forward.

"I believe, Your Royal Highness," he said in a low voice, "that you could help His Majesty."

"Help him?"

38

"First, to bring about peace in Luthenia."

"There is trouble there?"

Now Mr. Donington looked surprised.

"I felt sure Her Majesty the Queen would have told you."

"I am not very ... clear about exactly what is ... happening," Xenia replied.

"There are a great number of riots amongst the students and the workers, and overall there is a kind of national dissatisfaction."

He hesitated, then said frankly:

"It could, if such feelings get out of hand, prove a danger to the Monarchy itself."

"You mean the King might have to abdicate?"

"That is something I do not visualise for the moment," Mr. Donington said hastily, "and I know that if such a catastrophe should happen, Great Britain would be both distressed and alarmed."

He looked at Xenia, then said:

"That is why, Your Royal Highness, anything even approaching such a national disaster must be avoided."

"I understand," Xenia said in a low voice. "And thank you, Mr. Donington, for being so frank with me."

"If I have said anything to perturb Your Royal Highness, you must forgive me."

"I asked you for the truth, and I am glad that you have been so outspoken."

"You are very gracious," Mr. Donington said as he bowed.

When she thought over what she had heard, Xenia told herself that it would be a disaster for the King to lose his throne and for Luthenia to cease to be independent.

Her mother had talked to her about the previous King, who had been a friend of her grandfather. She had said that of all the small countries in the Balkans, in her opinion Luthenia was one of the most beautiful.

"There are high, snow-capped mountains, Xenia," she said, "fertile valleys with silver rivers running through them, and the people smile and look happy."

39

Barbara Cartland

It was a contrast, Xenia knew, to Serbia, which her mother had not liked, and to Bosnia, which had been uncomfortable with its glum people and quite inedible food.

She wished now that she had learnt more about Luthenia. But she decided that in the very short time she would be there she would do everything possible to find out what was wrong and warn Johanna.

When they stopped at Vienna, Xenia longed for a chance to see the beautiful Empress, whom everybody admired but who, she had been told, led a miserable, unhappy life in the austere Hapsburg Palace, tyrannised over by her formidable mother-in-law.

As she thought of her she realised that she had never asked about King István's parents.

At the first opportunity she cleverly brought the subject round to the Queen Mother.

"Tell me, Madame," she said to her lady-in-waiting, "about King István's mother."

"Oh, I wish you had known her, Your Royal Highness," Madame Gyula replied. "She was a very lovely and charming person."

This told Xenia that she was dead, and in the same way she discovered that the King had no brothers or sisters as he had been an only child.

"It was a great sadness," Madame Gyula said, "and the whole country is hoping that the King will have a large family."

She had spoken without thinking, and then she looked nervously at Xenia to see if she was annoyed.

"I have also found it very lonely being an only child," Xenia said, to set the elderly woman's mind at rest.

"I am sure you have, Your Royal Highness, but you will be happy in Luthenia, and everybody will be longing to entertain you and make you feel at home."

Xenia was careful not to speak to Madame Gyula about the situation in the country, but when they reached Vienna, Mr. Donington said good-bye and his place was taken by Count Gáspar Horváth.

Because of the short notice of her summons to leave England, it had not been possible for King István to send the Foreign Minister to London to escort her, as Xenia understood would have happened under ordinary circumstances.

Instead, Count Gáspar was waiting with the Royal Train, and Mr. Donington handed her over secretly, Xenia thought, as if she were a diplomatic bag!

She was at first more interested in the train than in the Count.

Her mother had told her that Queen Victoria had a special train in which she travelled, and with the increase of railways all over Europe many Monarchs had copied her example.

King István's train was, Xenia decided, exactly like a toy one.

It was white, with the Royal Coat-of-Arms emblazoned on it in colour, and the attendants who travelled on it wore a special gold and white uniform.

There was a Drawing-Room filled with flowers and several carriages to carry those in attendance.

As soon as she said good-bye to Mr. Donington and thanked him for looking after her, Count Gáspar explained how extremely upset the King and everybody else in the Palace at Molnár had been when they heard of the railway accident in which she had been involved.

"It was rather frightening at the time," Xenia said, "but I was very fortunate not to be hurt, except that occasionally I find myself forgetting things."

"That is to be expected, Your Royal Highness, but you will soon feel well again when you reach Luthenia."

"I hope so," Xenia replied.

She waited for an appropriate moment before saying to the Count:

"I understand there has been some trouble in the Capital."

She thought the Count glanced at her sharply, as if he wondered how much she knew.

He was a man of about forty-five, with grey hair, and she felt that while he appeared to spend a great deal of his time in attendance on the King, he was also a sportsman and undoubtedly a good rider.

"The Luthenians," her mother had said, "are all of course magnificent horsemen, which is characteristic of those with Hungarian blood."

She gave a little sigh as she said:

"Oh, dearest, I only wish Papa could buy you a really good horse to ride like the ones I had when I was at home."

"We are fortunate, Mama," Xenia said, "that the farmers are so fond of Papa that they let him ride their horses."

"Your father is a very good rider," her mother answered. "In fact he does everything well, but . . ."

She paused, and Xenia had said teasingly:

"I really believe, Mama, you are going to admit there are men in the Balkans who are better riders than Papa!"

"It is a different sort of riding," her mother said quickly. "The Hungarians, Slovians, and Luthenians spend almost their whole life in the saddle, and I have ridden since I was three years old."

"Do you miss it very much, Mama?"

"Sometimes I dream that I am galloping over the Steppes," her mother admitted, "but I promise you that as long as your father has a horse to ride I am content to stay at home."

As she grew older Xenia realised that however unselfish her mother might wish to be, when she saw a fine horse or watched other people riding well-bred animals, there was a yearning look in her eyes.

When they were alone she often talked to her daughter and described the feats of riding she had seen when she was a girl, the way the Slovians broke in the wild horses, and the magnificent collection of animals which had filled her grandfather's stables.

The Count was attempting to answer Xenia's question.

Love Leaves at Midnight

"There is a little trouble in Molnár, Your Royal Highness, but I am certain that the people only need to have their minds diverted from their mostly imaginary troubles for them to be forgotten."

'That is why Johanna has been sent for in a hurry to Luthenia,' Xenia silently decided.

Since she—or rather her cousin—had not been there since she and the King became engaged, there would obviously be presentations, Receptions, and perhaps a Ball.

It was exciting to Xenia to think that she might just for once in her life attend a State Ball.

Her mother had often described them to her, but she had never attended a Ball of any sort, State or otherwise.

She had been astonished when they reached Dover to see the enormous amount of luggage that Johanna carried with her, which had fortunately been retrieved undamaged from the wreckage of the train.

The luggage-van had not turned over and there had been no difficulty in transferring the big leather trunks to a second carriage, which was to follow the one in which Xenia travelled to the port.

She was almost speechless when she saw what the trunks Johanna was using on the train journey contained.

There were gowns that she had never dreamt of seeing, let alone being able to wear. They were so beautiful, so fragile, and so exquisite that Xenia was almost afraid to put them on in case she should spoil them.

"I must be very, very careful," she admonished herself, but it was a delight to see her reflection in the mirror and know that she did in fact look like a Fairy Princess.

All the colours had been chosen especially to accentuate the red of Johanna's hair, which was exactly like her own.

The only difference between them, Xenia thought, was that perhaps her skin was whiter and

43

had a little more of the magnolia look which her father had admired.

There were not only gowns for her to wear but a huge jewel-case filled with what appeared to be the King's treasury of jewels.

She had with difficulty prevented herself from exclaiming at their magnificence when Madame Gyula opened it for her.

"It is very fortunate," the lady-in-waiting said, "that I was in charge of this, Your Royal Highness, rather than your poor maid. If they had been lost it would have been a tragedy!"

"It would indeed," Xenia said, looking at the necklaces of pearls and diamonds and the bracelets to match, which were in another tray.

"I understand that some of them belong to your dear mother," Madame continued, "so it would have been a double loss had they been stolen or crushed in that terrible disaster."

Xenia could not help smiling a little to herself.

With every mile they travelled toward Luthenia the train accident was assuming larger and larger proportions in Madame Gyula's mind.

Xenia was quite certain that once they arrived, Madame was determined to play the heroine and doubtless would be surrounded by a rapturous audience while she recounted her traumatic experience!

One thing which was lucky was that it took her mind off her charge, and Xenia was able, since Madame's mind was elsewhere, to prevent her noticing several little lapses and mistakes she made.

The King's train travelled swiftly. At the same time it was a day and a night's journey to Luthenia from Vienna.

As they sped through Austria, Xenia found it difficult to do anything but stare out the window, entranced by everything she saw.

This was where she had always longed to be, in the part of Europe to which her mother belonged and which she had never thought for one instant she would be able to visit except in the poorest, most economical manner.

To be waited on in comfort beyond anything she had ever imagined was an irrepressible excitement, and to know also that every time she looked in the mirror she appeared more beautiful than she had ever been in her whole life was an unbelievable enchantment.

"But I am a Cinderella," she warned herself, "and at midnight I have to disappear! Only in this story my Fairy Godmother takes my place."

Sometimes when she was thinking about Johanna she wondered what it was like to be alone with a man one loved, hiding with him because they must not be seen together, but content, as Johanna had said, just to be in his arms.

Then, because the thought of her cousin's behaviour continued to shock her, she tried not to think about anything except what lay ahead.

They travelled through a high mountain pass, then crossed a bridge over a wide river, and were now within an hour's journey of the Luthenian border.

"You must... tell me what I am to... expect," she said to the Count with a sudden touch of panic.

"It will be nothing at all frightening, Your Royal Highness," he replied, as if he was surprised at her tone of voice. "You will receive an address of welcome frm the Mayor and the Foreign Minister will join the train. You know Mr. Miklos Dudich."

Xenia put her hand up to her forehead.

"You will think it very stupid, Count," she said, "but ever since the accident I have been finding difficulty in remembering some people. Tell me about Mr. Dudich."

"You will recognise him when you see him," the Count answered. "It was he who made all the arrangements regarding the announcement of your engagement to His Majesty when he stayed with your grandfather in Slovia."

"Yes, yes, of course," Xenia said. "How stupid of

45

me. These lapses of memory are quite frightening."

"It is quite a usual thing to happen," the Count said soothingly. "I remember when I had concussion after a bad fall out riding I lost my memory for two weeks."

"Then you will understand how foolish I feel," Xenia said with a smile. "And please help me in case I forget any of the protocol in Molnár. I believe His Majesty is very insistent that it should be correct."

The Count looked sceptical.

"If I am honest, Ma'am, I would like His Majesty to be far more particular about such things."

"You would?" Xenia asked surprised. "But Madame Gyula . . ."

The Count laughed.

"Madame is one of those people, Your Royal Highness, who are always in a flutter in case she should do the wrong thing, and therefore she exaggerates everything that is expected of her."

"I was becoming quite frightened in case I made mistakes and got into . . . trouble."

"If you are ever in any trouble, Your Royal Highness, any Luthenian from the King to his lowliest subject would forgive you," the Count said with an unmistakable expression of admiration in his eyes.

"I hope you are right," Xenia said doubtfully.

"I will do everything in my power to remind you of what is expected," the Count said, "but the Luthenians who met you in your own country reported that you were so assured, so polished in everything you said and did, that you might be ten years older than you really are."

Xenia felt her heart give a frightened leap.

The Luthenians and especially their King would not find her at all polished or experienced! She could only pray fervently that by some miracle she would be saved from making a fool of herself.

She passed through the ordeal at the frontier with what she thought to herself was flying colours, then they carried her on towards Molnár.

Now she had to meet the King.

It gave her a little more confidence when before they neared Molnár she put on one of Johanna's most beautiful gowns.

It was of pale green, the colour of the buds in spring, and the chic little hat that went with it was decorated with spring flowers.

When she was dressed, Xenia stared at herself in the mirror and she wished her mother could see her.

Now she understood why Mrs. Sandon had always regretted that her daughter would never wear the type of gown she herself had worn as a girl.

"Perhaps it would be a bore always to be so dressed up," Xenia tried to console herself.

Then she knew it would never be a bore to dress as she was now and to know without conceit that she looked exceedingly beautiful.

"We are nearly there, Your Royal Highness," Madame Gyula said in a fluttering tone from the door.

Looking at her reflection in the mirror, Xenia saw her eyes widen and they seemed very large in her pale face.

'It is all right. He will think you are Johanna. All you have to do is to be pleasant,' she thought to herself, almost in the tone of a School-Mistress instructing a pupil.

At the same time, as she turned to walk into the Drawing-Room she knew that her lips were dry and her hands were trembling a little.

She had already learnt that when they arrived, the King, who would be waiting at the station, would meet her alone in the train.

Madame Gyula, the Count, and the Foreign Minister whom she had greeted effusively would not be in attendance, and the curtains would be drawn so that there would be no prying eyes to see them greet each other.

As she entered the Drawing-Room to find that the lights were lit, Xenia wondered with a sudden tension if perhaps the King would kiss her.

After all, he was engaged to Johanna and engaged couples did kiss each other.

She had never been kissed and she thought frantically that Johanna was experienced in this as in other things and perhaps she might make a mistake.

"Supposing he notices and thinks it strange?" Xenia asked herself.

Then she remembered that Johanna had told her that she and the King had already arranged to go their own ways once they were married, in which case he was unlikely to be demonstrative.

It was a consoling thought. At the same time, as the train drew very slowly up to the station platform and Xenia could hear at first cheers, then the sound of a Band, she knew that she was trembling.

"I shall be waiting outside the carriage, Your Royal Highness, to greet His Majesty," Madame Gyula said, "so if there is anything you want, anything I can get you . . . ?"

"No, thank you," Xenia replied.

She was sitting stiffly on the edge of one of the arm-chairs, and the Count glanced at her with some concern in his eyes.

"Are you all right, Your Royal Highness?" he enquired. "Would you like me to fetch you a glass of water or a glass of wine? I realise that any ceremony is somewhat of a strain after all you have been through on the journey here."

"No, I am quite all right, thank you, Count," Xenia managed to say.

She did not sound particularly sure of it, but there was no time to say more.

The train drew to a halt and the Count and the Foreign Minister hurried through the door.

Again there were cheers and the sound of music, then voices which meant that the King was greeting those who had escorted her on the train.

Slowly, with her heart beating in an uncomfortable manner, Xenia rose to her feet.

She told herself that she must behave absolutely naturally and remember that she was Johanna, assured and sophisticated.

This would mean nothing to her, not even the moment when she was reunited with the man to whom she was engaged.

The door of the carriage opened and the King came in.

Although she had thought about him so much, although she had tried to find out everything she could about him, she had not expected him to look so impressive or indeed so different from any other man she had seen before.

He stood looking at her. He was wearing a white tunic which was covered in medals, and dark red trousers, and he carried a plumed hat.

Almost before he moved towards her she saw that he had the grace which her mother had described to her as part of their Hungarian heritage.

But it was his face, and the expression on it, which held her eyes.

He was dark-haired and good-looking—in fact he was extremely handsome—but never, Xenia thought, had she seen on a young man's face such an expression of cynicism combined with an aloof indifference that seemed to make him look as if he was scornful of everything and everybody.

Yet she found that his dark eyes were strangely penetrating, and as he looked at her she felt as if he searched for something beneath the surface which he was quite certain he would not find.

He had reached her side before with an effort she remembered that she should curtsey to him.

As she did so, he took her hand in his, and must have realised that her fingers were very cold and trembling.

"Welcome to Luthenia, Xenia," he said. "I deeply regret to hear that you had such an unfortunate experience before you left England."

Rising from her curtsey, she looked up at him. Then, because she was more shy than she had imagined she could be, her eyes flickered and she looked away.

"I was very ... fortunate ... not to be ... injured," she said.

"The Count tells me that you were unconscious for a time. You must have been hit on the head."

Xenia knew he had heard this from Mr. Donington, and because she thought it would excuse anything she did that might seem unusual she replied:

"I am all ... right now ... at least I ... think so."

The King released her hand.

"Shall I tell you that despite what you have suffered you look extremely beautiful? Your gown and bonnet are very becoming."

"Thank ... you."

Despite every resolution to behave naturally, Xenia could not prevent the colour from rising in her cheeks.

It was not only that she was unused to compliments, it was the fact that the King was looking at her with his penetrating, dark eyes, and his voice was deeper than she had expected it to be.

Something in his tone made her feel as if she listened to him not only with her ears but also with her heart.

"Well, we should have been here long enough to satisfy the sentimental yearnings of the populace for romance," the King said abruptly in a different tone. "Are you ready to go?"

He spoke so differently from the manner in which he had just been speaking that Xenia looked at him in surprise. Then she said quickly:

"Yes ... of course. I am quite ... ready."

The King opened the door and Madame Gyula and the Count came hurrying in.

"Let us get on with it, Horváth," the King said. "And I hope there are enough soldiers on the route."

Xenia heard what he said but not the Count's

answer, and she had no time to ask what it meant, because the King was obviously impatient.

They stepped out onto the platform, the Guard of Honour came to attention, the Band struck up the National Anthem, and they stood side by side on a red carpet until it was finished.

Cheers broke out from the crowd who were in the station, although Xenia realised they were all persons of importance who had been specially invited to be present.

A number of dignitaries were presented to her. Then they moved through the Guard of Honour and out of the station to a waiting carriage.

She and the King were to travel alone in an open landau drawn by six grey horses, three of them ridden by postillions in elaborate gold uniforms.

She remembered her mother telling her how she had behaved when she lived at home in Slovia, so Xenia waved her hand to the crowd and smiled.

Her mother had said once:

"Your grandmother used to think it familiar and undignified to smile, and my father felt the same, but Dorottyn and I always smiled and waved. We felt something was wrong if the people in the crowd did not smile back."

"I am sure they loved you, Mama," Xenia said.

"Dorottyn and I used to believe they did," Mrs. Sandon replied, "but sometimes I have wondered if Royalty like ourselves should have given more to the people. They do so much for us, and perhaps we could have helped them in a dozen different ways. A smile is a poor return for a lifetime of service."

Her mother spoke very seriously and Xenia had not really understood or troubled her head about what she was saying.

Now her words came back and Xenia smiled and waved as she thought a Princess should do, and she felt, although she was not sure, that the crowd was pleased.

The King made no effort to acknowledge the

cheers but lay back in a corner of the carriage, looking, Xenia thought, as if he was bored with the whole
proceeding.

It was difficult for her to take her eyes from the
crowd and look at the buildings they were passing,
but she did notice that the trees which lined the
roadways were colourful with blossoms.

"It is very beautiful," she exclaimed.

"Beautiful?" the King questioned. "I remember
your saying that my country was small and insignifi-
cant, and that if you had the choice you would prefer
to live in France or England."

Xenia did not reply, but she wondered how Johanna could have been so disagreeable about the
country over which she was to reign.

The horses turned off a Square which was
crowded with people and into another road.

There were cheers and hand-waving for the
first half of it, then suddenly the noise seemed to die
down and the carriage moved a little quicker.

Still waving, Xenia saw a large number of un-
smiling faces watching them in silence.

They carried banners inscribed with words she
could not at first read, then some larger ones, and the
rest caught her eye.

She read:

DOWN-TRODDEN AND DESPISED!

She read the words in astonishment, and saw
another, saying:

WE DEMAND JUSTICE!

Because there was no response to her waving
hand she dropped it into her lap.

"What is wrong?" she asked the King. "Who are
these people?"

"A lot of revolutionary students," he answered.
"Ignore them."

Almost as if they heard his words, the students
suddenly broke out into loud boos. They were also
shouting and yelling in a manner which was obviously meant to be offensive.

The coachman whipped up the horses and they were travelling much more quickly than before.

But the hostile atmosphere on either side of them seemed to increase and Xenia felt afraid.

She remembered stories she had been told ever since she was a child of assassins who were pledged to exterminate the aristocracy and anarchists who threw bombs at Monarchs.

Because it was so menacing and so unexpected, without really thinking what she was doing, she put out her hand and slipped it into the King's.

"Would they . . . hurt us?" she asked.

He looked at the fear in her eyes in surprise, then he answered:

"They are only trying to make a nuisance of themselves. I should have warned you this might happen."

Too late Xenia remembered that her mother had always told her that Royal Personages never showed fear.

She had often told stories of how brave Kings and Queens were, even when bombs hit their carriages and killed their horses.

'I am behaving like the commoner I am,' Xenia thought.

At the same time, she still held on to the King's hand because it was comforting.

A few seconds later the students were left behind and once again there were crowds of cheering, waving people, mostly women and children.

Then just ahead of them, built on the hill and approached by a wide street bordered with flowering trees, Xenia saw the Palace.

It looked exactly as she thought a Palace should look, impressive and romantic, with turrets on either side of it and gold-tipped, wrought-iron gates in front.

She had taken her hand from the King's when she had started to wave once again to the crowd. Now, her fears forgotten, she turned to him with shining eyes.

53

"It is just the sort of Palace a King ought to live in," she said. "It is exactly right and it is as beautiful and impressive as your beautiful country."

As she spoke she raised her head to where towering directly above the Palace there was a mountain and beyond it along the whole valley a large range of them, some far away in the distance, still snow-capped from the previous winter.

"It is lovely!" Xenia cried. "Lovely, lovely, lovely! How could anyone fail to be happy here?"

"And do you think that is what you will be?" the King asked in a tone of doubt that was unmistakable.

His words were like a splash of cold water against her face.

Too late Xenia realised that she had been speaking not as Johanna but as herself, and saying what she, Xenia...a counterfeit, fake Princess...really thought.

Chapter Three

There was a big crowd outside the Palace, but as Xenia waved to them she realised that perhaps only one in three was responding.

The rest, who were mostly men, stood with their arms crossed and surly expressions on their faces.

She wanted to ask the King what was wrong with them, but she knew she would not make her voice heard, and the next moment they had entered the gold-tipped gates which were guarded by soldiers.

There seemed to be an unnecessary amount of them at the gates and in the court-yard, besides being stationed up the long flight of steps which led to the front door.

They looked very smart in their red tunics and dark blue trousers, and the officers with gold epaulettes on their shoulders and wearing their medals were most impressive.

Xenia and the King walked up the red-carpeted steps, then entered one of the loveliest Entrance-Halls she had ever seen.

It was of white, with Corinthian columns touched with gold, and it had an exquisitely painted ceiling. There were a number of statues which Xenia saw at once were exceptionally well sculpted.

But there was no time to see anything more before they were led by a number of officials down a wide corridor and into a huge Reception-Room.

This again was quite entrancing, and at first Xenia could only see the huge crystal chandeliers reflected and rereflected on either side of the long room.

As she and the King moved through a throng of people towards a dais at the far end on which there were two gold thrones, it flashed through her mind that the room had in fact been copied in general plan from the Hall of Mirrors at the Palace of Versailles.

'It is very beautiful!' she thought appreciatively.

Then it was impossible to think of anything except the people who were being presented to her.

First there were several aged relatives of the King, who, she gathered, were staying in the Palace to chaperon her, then there were the Members of the Government.

The Prime Minister was an elderly man with grey hair, but there was something in his bearing and the expression on his face which told Xenia he was a force to be reckoned with.

He murmured a few words of welcome before he presented his Cabinet one by one.

Xenia felt that they looked at her appraisingly as if they were summing up in their minds whether she would be useful or otherwise.

Then she told herself she was being imaginative.

In Luthenia, as in other small countries, the Monarch was in control and only in exceptional instances did the Government not accept his decision as binding.

There were so many people to meet that after a few moments she felt bemused and it was impossible to distinguish one face from another. She could merely reply to the greetings that were offered to her in what she hoped were gracious sentences of gratitude.

When they first entered the room she had felt so

shy as to be unable to say anything, and wanted more than anything else to hide herself.

Then she remembered not only that she was supposed to be Johanna but also that her mother had always said:

"Shyness is selfish. It means you are thinking of yourself. Think of other people and their troubles, not your own."

That was what Xenia now tried to do, and when the Reception was over and the guests applauded, although it was a dignified and restrained gesture, she felt she had been successful.

She and the King left and they walked up the stairs to what she guessed would be their private apartments.

She had to keep remembering that she was supposed to have visited Luthenia before, but she gathered from some of the things that were said that it was some time before the King and Johanna had become betrothed.

"These rooms have been redecorated," the King said, "and I hope the result will please you."

He spoke as if he would be surprised if they did.

But when they entered the Sitting-Room decorated in the French style and furnished with Louis XIV console-tables and mirrors, Xenia could only stare round in delight.

The Palace at Slovia had contained some fine antique furniture which her mother had not only described to Xenia but had also explained to her the different periods in history from which it had come.

Her grandfather had also been a collector of pictures and Xenia was quite knowledgeable on the Italian Masters and on the primitives.

It was one thing to learn about such treasures, but very different to actually see them.

"That is a Fragonard I am sure!" she exclaimed.

She was looking at a picture on one wall which had an ethereal beauty about it, so compelling that it

seemed almost to affect the atmosphere of the room
itself.

"It is one of my favourites," the King said. "It
seemed right for this room, although I remember that
you were not particularly interested in paintings."

"How could anyone not appreciate this?" Xenia
asked, looking at the gentle lines of the picture and
the exquisite blending of the colours.

There was also a Boucher over which she went
into ecstasies, and it was hard to look from the pictures at the china which had been arranged on the
inlaid tables.

"I am glad you appreciate this room, for it will
be yours," the King said. "At the same time, I am
afraid you cannot spend much time here at the moment. The Prime Minister wishes to speak with you
as soon as you have had a short rest."

"The Prime Minister?" Xenia enquired.

"He wishes to tell you why you have been asked
to come here with such precipitate haste."

"Surely you can tell me that?" Xenia replied.

She looked at the King as she spoke and she
thought as she did so that he seemed more cynical
and more bored than ever.

'What has made him like that?' she wondered.

Then as she met his eyes she felt that he was
looking at her as searchingly as she was looking at
him.

It was just an impression. Then abruptly he said:

"I hope you enjoyed yourself in England."

"It . . . it was very . . . pleasant," Xenia replied
quickly.

"Pleasant?"

He made the word sound like a sneer.

"Surely your English lover should have made it
more delightful than that?"

Xenia was very still. Then because of the tone in
the King's voice and also because the word "lover"
disturbed her, the colour flared in her cheeks.

She could think of nothing to say in answer, so

she turned aside to walk to the window, and because she felt agitated she took off her little hat as she did so.

She stood looking out but not seeing the formal garden below or the fountains playing in the centre of it.

She was trying wildly to think of what Johanna would say in the circumstances and feeling instead that her brain could not think clearly, as if it were stuffed with cotton-wool.

The sunshine turned her hair into a fiery red, and her skin was very white.

"No reply?" the King asked mockingly from behind her. "Was it too ecstatic to describe in words? Or was it perhaps disappointing, as love-affairs so often can be?"

Still Xenia did not answer, and after a moment he said:

"If your experiences are too private to be related, surely you are interested in mine? You have not yet enquired after Elga. I felt sure you would be interested in my association with her."

Now he was jeering, and quite suddenly, without really thinking what she was saying, Xenia said:

"Please . . . do not . . . talk like . . . that."

"Why not?"

"Because it . . . spoils everything. It is so beautiful . . . here in a . . . Palace out of a fairy-tale . . . and I want to . . . enjoy it . . . for . . ."

She nearly added, "the next few days," then prevented herself, so that her voice died away on the last word like an unfinished piece of music.

For a moment there was complete silence. Then the King said in a different tone:

"After what you said to me the last time we met, I find your attitude difficult to understand."

Xenia drew in her breath.

She must not let Johanna down, she thought. At the same time, she could not bear the short time she would be in the Palace to be spoilt.

59

Just for once in her life she would be of importance, part of the life that her mother had described to her.

Every second must be treasured in her mind so that when she was back in England, looking for employment, with only Johanna's fee and what her father had left between her and starvation, she could remember it.

As the King did not speak, she turned round to look at him, her eyes very large and a little frightened.

Suppose she had said too much? Suppose he suspected that she was not who she pretended to be?

He was certainly staring at her with a penetration which made her feel shy. Then, as she waited, unexpectedly he smiled.

It transformed his face. He looked younger and even more handsome, and certainly more human.

"For the first time, Xenia," he said, "you seem to be your age instead of the sophisticated, blasé woman of the world that you have appeared to be in the past."

Xenia felt a quick surge of relief. He was not suspicious! She managed to say lightly:

"No-one could be blasé in such beautiful surroundings."

She moved from the window as she spoke and was aware that the King was watching her.

"Do you want me to change before I meet the Prime Minister?" she enquired.

"No, of course not," he said. "Perhaps you would like to tidy yourself. Your bed-room is next door and your maids will be waiting for you there."

"Thank you," Xenia answered. "Then shall I come back here?"

"I will collect you in twenty minutes' time."

"Thank you," she said again.

She was not certain if she ought to curtsey before leaving the King but decided it would be better to be formal than otherwise.

She therefore curtseyed, feeling that it was impossible to be anything but graceful in her exquisite green gown.

Then without looking at the King again she opened the door which she was certain would lead into her bed-room and was aware as she did so that he was standing in the centre of the Sitting-Room, watching her.

There were two maids in the room, which Xenia saw at a glance was as attractive as the one she had just left.

The huge bed, carved and gilded, was draped with soft blue silk curtains which matched the inset panels on the walls.

Once again there was a ceiling exquisitely painted, and the furniture was painted too and carved with flowers and fruit which Xenia knew was traditionally Austrian.

The whole room was so beautiful that she could only look about her until she realised that the two maids were curtseying low and waiting for her to notice them.

Without thinking that it might seem a strangely English custom, Xenia held out her hand to the elder woman.

"It is nice to meet you," she said, "and thank you for doing my unpacking."

"It is an honour and a privilege, Your Royal Highness," the maid replied.

"You must tell me your name."

"It is Margit, Your Royal Highness, and this is Vilma."

Vilma was young and attractive and obviously extremely impressed with her new mistress.

She made a series of nervous little curtseys and Xenia smiled and walked to the dressing-table to tidy her hair.

"Do you wish to change your gown, Your Royal Highness?" Margit asked.

"It is unnecessary . . ." Xenia began to say.

Then she glanced at the open wardrobe and saw that it was already half-filled with gowns which might have come in her dreams.

She suddenly had an irresistible urge to try on every one of them and wear them before her Cinderella story came to an end when midnight sent her back in her rags to the kitchen.

"Yes, I will change," she said with a lilt in her voice. "Which do you think would be the most suitable for this time of the day?"

"There is a banquet in the Palace tonight," Margit answered, "and I thought Your Royal Highness would wish to wear a white gown—perhaps this one."

She drew from the wardrobe a gown of white silk, the front draped almost Grecian-fashion and caught up at the sides with bunches of yellow lilies, before the back, with only the faintest suggestion of a bustle, fell to the floor in a small train.

It was so lovely that there was a perceptible pause before Xenia said:

"Yes, I am sure that would be the correct gown to wear tonight."

"Then I suggest Your Royal Highness change now into this one," Margit said.

She took down a gown of the palest eau-de-nile-coloured silk trimmed with lace dyed to the same shade.

When she put it on Xenia thought that it became her even more than the gown she had worn previously, and yet it was hard to decide which one was lovelier.

It was fortunate that she and Joanna were the same height and the only difference was that she was more slender and therefore slightly smaller in the waist.

However, many of the gowns she noticed had belts, and the ones without them could easily be taken in and let out again later.

'The servants will think it is the accident that has made me lose weight,' she decided.

Therefore, as she dressed she told Margit what had happened and how frightening it had been.

"A terrible experience, Your Royal Highness!" the elderly woman murmured, while Vilma listened with the look on her face of a child who has been taken to a Pantomime.

"Trains are dangerous things," Margit went on, "but perhaps those in England are not as good as ours."

Because she spoke of England it brought vividly back to Xenia's mind the way in which the King had spoken to her of her English "lover."

She had been right, she decided, in thinking that he was shocked and perhaps disgusted by the idea of his wife, the future Queen, behaving as Johanna was doing.

'How could she have been so stupid as to let him know?' Xenia wondered silently.

Then she thought that perhaps it would have been even more reprehensible to deceive him.

It was a problem such as she had never imagined would concern her, and she found herself puzzling once again over her cousin's behaviour.

However, she told herself severely, it was none of her business.

All she had to do was to keep the King happy and unsuspicious and, perhaps more important, try to help him as Mr. Donington had said she should.

The idea made her feel nervous. She was sure that nothing she could say or do would be of the least consequence to him.

He was so magnificent, so important, Xenia thought. Then she told herself that, whatever else he was, he was obviously not happy.

Her mother had once said when they were talking of her life as a girl:

"Ordinary people always think that those who live in Palaces have a charmed life of ease and happiness. That is not true."

"You were not happy, Mama?"

"Only when I was very young," her mother re-

63

plied. "When I grew older I often felt frustrated at being shut away from reality."

Mrs. Sandon had laughed before she added:

"I felt like a canary in a cage or a goldfish in a bowl, there to be stared at but not to participate in what was happening round me."

She paused before she went on:

"If I had not run away with your father I should just have lived an empty, meaningless existence, with a broken heart."

"You would have made a very beautiful Arch-Duchess, Mama," Xenia said.

"I know one thing quite surely," Mrs. Sandon replied. "I should have been a very unhappy wife of the Arch-Duke, and a very dull one."

As if she felt she must explain her last remark she added:

"When people are unhappy they are either dull and bored or bitter and disillusioned. It is then that they are at their worst."

"I can understand that, Mama."

"I want you to understand it. Happiness is important not only to the development of one's self but to everyone with whom one comes in contact."

It was happiness, Xenia thought now, that her mother had tried to give to the people of Little Coombe, and it was not surprising that everybody in the village had adored her.

She remembered how many tears had been shed at her mother's funeral and how even the poorest villagers had brought flowers to lay on her grave.

'The King is unhappy,' she thought. 'I must try to make him happy as Mama would have done.'

She did not ask for the moment how such a thing was possible in so short a time. She only knew that it was as if she had been set a task and somehow, however impossible it seemed, she must make an effort to get it done.

When she went from her bed-room back into the Sitting-Room the King was waiting for her.

He was standing looking at a newspaper as she entered and at the sound of the door he turned round. Almost instinctively Xenia stood still and waited as if for his approval.

There was a little pause, then he said:

"Very attractive! You look even more beautiful than you did half an hour ago. Is that what you expect me to say?"

He was not jeering or mocking her; in fact there was a faint smile on his lips as if he realised why she had changed.

"I do not wish to be put to ... shame by your ... Palace," Xenia explained.

"You could never do anything but adorn it," the King answered.

Xenia smiled.

"That is the nicest compliment anyone could possibly pay me."

She spoke excitedly, then wondered if he would expect her to be blasé in regard to compliments; for after all, Johanna must have had so many.

Then she suddenly felt impatient with trying to remember Johanna and to choose everything she said and did with care, in case later the King should notice that there was a difference between them.

'If he does,' Xenia silently told herself, 'there will be nothing he can do about it. And I shall not be here, so it will not worry me.'

Almost as if someone had told her what to do, she decided that if she was to help the King she must be herself.

"Do show me what other alterations you have made to the Palace," she said aloud, "for to tell you the truth, the accident I had on the train seems to have affected my memory so that I cannot remember exactly what it was like when I came here last."

"What else do you find it hard to remember?" the King questioned.

"An awful lot," Xenia answered. "Count Gáspar

65

was telling me that when he had concussion he lost his memory for a fortnight. I feel that the same thing has happened to me; so perhaps in two weeks I shall be back to normal."

"That would be a pity," the King said, "because, accident or not, I like you as you are."

"Then you must help me," Xenia said, "because I am finding it impossible to remember whom I have met before and whom I have not, and I would hate anyone to think that I had forgotten them."

"Would their feelings really matter to you?" the King enquired.

"But of course they would," Xenia said. "I should hate to be unkind, or that people should think I was cold or indifferent."

She told herself as she spoke that that was how he had looked when they first met, and somehow in the future she had to prevent him from showing himself in such a bad light to the crowds who had come to cheer him.

Surprisingly, he guessed what she was thinking and said:

"Are you preaching to me in a somewhat obscure manner? If so, it is something I never expected."

"I would not ... presume to ... preach," Xenia said quickly.

"Nevertheless, I have a feeling that there is a pill hidden somewhere in the jam."

Xenia laughed.

"That is exactly how I was always given my medicine—in a spoonful of jam or honey."

"I was too," the King admitted, "and that is why I suspect that what you are offering me is going to taste very nasty."

He was far more perceptive, she thought, than she had expected him to be, and she thought it would be a mistake to be too obvious in what she was trying to do.

"Is the Prime Minister waiting for us?" she asked.

"I expect so," the King replied. "But there is no hurry. Let him wait!"

"Is that not rather . . . rude?"

"Any rudeness that Kalolyi gets from me is deserved," the King said almost savagely. "He undermines my authority, he usurps my power, and will, unless I can prevent it, sit on my throne."

He spoke violently and Xenia looked at him in surprise.

"If you feel like that about him," she said, "why do you not get rid of him?"

"And cause a Constitutional crisis?" the King asked, and added: "It is not a question of who would win the battle: Kalolyi is already the victor. I am not the King of this country—he is!"

Xenia began to understand why the King looked as he did.

"I heard that there was . . . trouble in the Capital," she said.

"Trouble? Of course there is trouble," the King replied.

"Is there nothing you can do?"

"Ask Kalolyi," the King answered. "He holds the reins. When things go right he takes the credit, and when they go wrong I get the blame."

His voice was angry, then he added:

"Why should you listen to this? Come and hear what Kalolyi has to say and learn what part you have to play in the chaos he has created."

Xenia looked at the King in surprise, but he moved towards the door and opened it, and she walked past him into the passage.

A Court Official was waiting to bow respectfully before he walked ahead of them down the Grand Staircase.

"Have all the guests left?" Xenia asked, seeking something to say.

She was aware that the official ahead of them could overhear everything they said.

"I imagine a number will still linger on," the King replied, "but we need not concern ourselves with them. Our meeting with the Prime Minister is in a different part of the Palace."

They walked down a number of wide passages.

There were pictures hung on the walls which Xenia longed to examine, and she hoped that while she was in the Palace she would have time to see everything.

'If only I could have a little model of the place,' she thought, 'almost like a doll's-house. Then it would be easy to remember every little detail and it would be always mine.'

Already she had the feeling that the minutes were ticking by too quickly and almost before she could begin to appreciate her surroundings she would be whisked away from them.

Flunkeys in the Royal livery opened huge double doors and the King and Xenia walked in through them side by side.

They were in a room which was more masculine and perhaps more businesslike than those Xenia had seen in the rest of the Palace, and there were three men waiting for them.

One, Xenia saw, was the Foreign Minister whom she had already met, another was the Prime Minister, and the other she vaguely remembered being presented to her at the Reception as the Lord Chancellor.

They bowed their heads and the King indicated a chair upholstered in green velvet on which Xenia could sit. Then as he sat down next to her he said:

"Please be seated, gentlemen."

The Prime Minister was facing Xenia, and as she waited a little apprehensively for what he had to say, he glanced at the King, then began:

"I expect Your Royal Highness has already been told—"

"I have said nothing!" the King interrupted. "I

left that to you, Prime Minister. It is your plan, and I thought you could explain it to her better than I."

There was a sarcastic note in his voice which Xenia disliked and which made her feel embarrassed, so she smiled at the Prime Minister and asked:

"You have something to tell me?"

"You may have wondered, Ma'am, why we asked you to come here from London with such haste."

"It was certainly unexpected," Xenia said.

"You have doubtless heard that we have trouble in Luthenia?"

"I was told that."

"I think therefore it is imperative that we divert the minds of the populace as quickly as possible."

"Divert them from what?" Xenia asked.

"Rebellion! Revolution!" the Prime Minister said sharply.

"If that happens, it will be your Government's doing," the King interrupted. "I have said for a long time that the taxes are too high and the people will not put up with so many petty restrictions forever."

"As I have informed Your Majesty on previous occasions," the Prime Minister answered, "my Government had no alternative but to enforce the laws to which you object."

"My objections certainly pass unheeded," the King said in a disagreeable tone.

The Prime Minister seemed about to answer him equally angrily. Then with an effort he changed his mind and said to Xenia:

"We asked Your Royal Highness to come here because, as I have said, it is important to take the people's minds off their imaginary grievances."

Xenia thought the King was once again ready to interrupt at the word "imaginary," but he merely threw himself back in his chair with the sulky attitude he had adopted in the carriage when they drove from the station.

"What are you suggesting I could do?" Xenia asked.

"I am arranging, Your Royal Highness," the Prime Minister answered, "that your marriage to His Majesty should take place immediately."

For a moment Xenia could only stare at him as if she could not comprehend what he had said.

Then in a voice that seemed to catch in her throat so that it was hardly audible she asked:

"Im-imme ... diately?"

"Within seven days, Your Royal Highness. It is to be announced tonight and the decorations will start going up in the streets tomorrow."

"I ... it is ... impossible!"

The words seemed almost to burst from Xenia's lips.

"Nothing is impossible," the Prime Minister replied, "and this, Ma'am, is imperative."

"But in a week!" Xenia exclaimed. "No! I cannot agree. We must wait a little ... longer than that."

She was trying as she spoke to calculate wildly how soon Johanna could be with her.

She had taken three days to reach Molnár and Johanna had arranged to spend ten days with Lord Gratton.

Supposing that if after that it took her three days to reach Luthenia, that would be thirteen days in all.

She saw that the Prime Minister was going to speak, and she said quickly:

"Two weeks ... I could manage in two weeks ... I think ... and I cannot imagine that a week will make much difference."

"It can take less than twenty-four hours, Your Royal Highness, for a country to be plunged into revolution and for a throne to be lost."

The Prime Minister spoke grimly, but Xenia had the idea that he was deliberately trying to frighten her.

She looked at the King and saw that he was sit-

ting back, obviously intending to take no further part
in the argument.

"Are you really saying that unless our ... marriage takes ... place in the next ... seven days, His
Majesty might lose his ... throne?"

It was difficult to speak calmly, but somehow
she managed it.

"I am saying, Your Royal Highness," the Prime
Minister replied, "that I consider it imperative that
you should be married next Tuesday, as I have arranged. What could be the point of waiting another
week?"

"But my ... father and mother could not be ...
present."

"That is indeed unfortunate," the Prime Minister allowed. "At the same time, I feel sure that His
Royal Highness, when he learns what has occurred,
will appreciate the urgency of the situation."

"Even if the wedding is ... announced, the ceremony need not take ... place until ... fourteen days
from now," Xenia said.

The Prime Minister made an expressive gesture
with his hands.

"Seven days—fourteen—what is the point of waiting? You are here in Molnár. I have everything organised, and His Majesty agreed before we sent to
England to ask Your Royal Highness to come here at
once."

"I agreed because you held a pistol at my head,"
the King remarked.

"And, having agreed, what is the point of arguing over a few days?" the Prime Minister enquired.

Xenia tried to think of an excuse and failed.

"Very well then. It is settled," the Prime Minister said. "The announcement will go out immediately
and will be in the newspapers tomorrow morning."

He paused but no-one spoke, and he went on:

"I have arranged that Your Royal Highness and
His Majesty will meet the Press tomorrow. They will
be at a Reception that is being given in Parliament,

then they can come to the Palace later, Ma'am, where they will wish to have more intimate details of you and doubtless of your trousseau."

There was a kind of sting in the Prime Minister's voice which Xenia did not like.

Indeed, she thought there was nothing she liked about the man, and she suspected that he bull-dozed everyone as he had bull-dozed her into agreeing to what he wanted.

The King rose to his feet.

"Doubtless, Kalolyi," he said, "you will be sending us a list of instructions which of course we shall be expected to fulfil to the letter."

His voice was both sarcastic and bitter.

"Your Majesty is most gracious!"

The animosity between the two men seemed to vibrate in the air, and to relieve the tension Xenia held out her hand to the Foreign Minister.

"It was so kind of you to come to the border to meet me, Mr. Dudich."

"It was a very great pleasure, Ma'am," he replied, "and may I express my regret that the Arch-Duke and the Arch-Duchess will be prevented from attending your wedding. I understand they are in Russia."

"I am sure when they learn of it they will be greatly disappointed," Xenia said.

She shook hands with the Prime Minister, feeling as she touched him that he was even more unpleasant than he appeared to be.

The King was right: the man was ambitious, overbearing, and undoubtedly had the makings of a dictator.

With a sense of relief Xenia saw an ingratiating, almost apologetic smile on the face of the Lord Chancellor. Then she and the King were walking across the room and out into the corridor.

They walked together in silence until he stopped at two beautifully painted doors which were hastily opened for them and she found herself in a Salon which had long windows opening into the garden.

As the door closed behind them the King said violently:

"Now you understand! Now you see what I am up against! It is entirely the Prime Minister's fault that there is talk of a revolution."

"The people cannot like him," Xenia replied.

"They fear him, which is more important, and his Cabinet are nothing but rabbits. He mesmerises them!"

"Then you must get rid of him," Xenia said.

The King laughed but there was no humour in the sound.

"I might as well try to push over one of the mountains single-handedly. He has got himself into the position where his word is law, and that doddering old Lord Chancellor agrees with everything he says."

"There must be a ... way," Xenia murmured.

The King looked at her, then said in a different tone:

"I am sorry to worry you with all this. After all, you have no wish to marry me any more than I wish to marry you, but Kalolyi has arranged our marriage as he has arranged everything else."

"Is there ... someone else you would ... wish to marry?" Xenia asked in a low voice.

"Good Lord, no!" the King said. "With Elga it is not a question of marriage, as you well know. But I do not wish to be pressurised by Kalolyi into doing anything. He had everything fixed up with your father without even consulting me!"

"I can see how appalling the whole ... thing must seem to you," Xenia said.

"You were certainly not very sympathetic when we talked about it before."

Xenia did not answer. Instead she said:

"There is no time to discuss what happened in

the past. We have to think of the future, and to find
some way in which you can break the Prime Minister's
hold over you and over the country."

As she spoke she thought to herself how hope-
less it seemed and how helpless she felt.

What did she know about Prime Ministers, revo-
lutions, or Kings for that matter?"

And yet, she thought to herself, tyrants, even
when they were petty ones like Mrs. Berkeley, were
all the same. They forced and crushed people into
subservience, leaving them without the power to escape.

"What are you thinking?" the King asked.

"I was thinking about you," Xenia replied, "and
wondering if you had perhaps given in too ... easily."

"What do you mean by that?"

"I wondered what was wrong when we drove
from the station and I thought ..."

She hesitated.

"Well—what did you think?" the King asked.

"You may think it ... rude."

He smiled faintly.

"I imagine you are going to be frank, and
would it reassure you if I say that however rude it
may be I will not take offence?"

"Well ... I thought that you looked ... bored
and aloof ... as if you considered all the people who
were cheering as we went along the route were too
far ... beneath you to be considered."

"Good God! It was not that!" the King ejacu-
lated. "If the truth were told, I was resenting the way
in which you had been sent for without my being
consulted. I was resenting having to marry you
whether I wanted to or not, and resenting too that the
people were cheering merely because they had been
told to do so."

"What do you mean ... they had been told to
do so?" Xenia asked.

"There have been Town Criers going through
the streets for the last three days heralding your ar-

rival, extolling your charms, telling the people not in words but by inference that everything will be changed once they have a Queen, and you know damned well that is not true!"

Xenia looked startled at the swear-word and the King said irritably:

"I apologise. I should not speak to you like that, but I am fed up with being in a treadmill from which I cannot escape and in which however fast I go it gets me nowhere."

He spoke so bitterly that Xenia was moved.

She took a step to his side and put her hand on his arm.

"I am sorry," she said, "very sorry. But I cannot believe there is not a way out waiting for you . . . if only we could . . . find it."

She spoke with a compassion that came from her very heart. Then as she looked up into the King's eyes it was impossible to look away.

They stood looking at each other, then the clock on the mantelpiece chimed.

Xenia looked away.

"What time am I to be . . . ready for the . . . banquet?" she asked.

"You have three-quarters of an hour."

She gave a little cry.

"Then I shall have to hurry."

She turned towards the door.

"Let them wait!" the King said. "I may sit at the head of the table, but Kalolyi will really be the host. It is he who has invited the guests."

Xenia had reached the door and she turned her head to smile at him.

"I do not intend to be late," she replied, "because I am hungry and I am quite certain that the food in the Palace will be delectable, as is everything else here."

She pulled open the door as she spoke, and as she went she heard the King laugh, but this time it was a sound of genuine amusement.

75

Chapter Four

Xenia awoke with a feeling of urgency, then
realised as she opened her eyes that she had several
reasons for anxiety.

First and foremost was the knowledge that she
might actually have to marry the King before Johanna
returned.

The possibility made her feel very alarmed.

Then she told herself sensibly that Johanna
would see the announcement of the King's forthcom-
ing marriage in the English newspapers and come to
Luthenia at once.

Xenia was quite certain that every newspaper in
Europe would carry the story that the King's marriage
would take place on the following Tuesday.

Editorials would be speculating on the need for
such haste and doubtless would attribute it to the
truth—that it was a palliative for the people.

At the same time, the thought of becoming the
King's legal wife while he imagined he was marrying
her cousin seemed to her too fantastic to contemplate.

But there was nothing she could do for the moment except to agree to the Prime Minister's plans, so
she set that problem on one side while she considered the difficulties which confronted the King.

She felt last night at her first State Banquet that
it was so exciting and so magnificent that she must in

her small way do something to prevent everything being spoilt by the dissatisfaction of the people in Luthenia.

It had been an enchantment she had never
known to talk to the Statesmen and noblemen who
were entertained at the Palace, and also to meet
the King's relations.

The nicest of them, she decided, was his aunt,
the Dowager Duchess Elizabeth of Mildenburg, who
reminded her of her mother and who was in fact a
distant relative of the King of Slovia.

The Dowager Duchess was horrified that the
marriage should take place while the Arch-Duke and
Arch-Duchess were in Russia.

"I am sure your mother will be very upset, my
dear," she said to Xenia.

"I am afraid so, Ma'am," Xenia replied. "But the
Prime Minister is insistent that it is the only way to
forestall the threat of revolution."

The Dowager Duchess gave her a glance which
told her she was surprised that Xenia dared to voice
the truth. Then she said:

"I am worried about István. You must help him,
dear, as only a wife can help a man in difficult times
like this."

"I will do my very best," Xenia promised, and
the Dowager Duchess smiled at her with approval.

The table, decorated with gold ornaments, exotic
flowers, and lit by huge gold candelabra, was more
beautiful than she could possibly have imagined.

She knew too that the gown she wore comple-
mented the scene and she thought, although she was
not sure, that the King's eyes rested on her appreciatively.

"I can understand," she told herself honestly
when she went to bed, "that Johanna cannot bear to
give all this up, not even for the man she loves."

At the same time, however alluring a throne
might be, Xenia was quite sure that if she were

in Johanna's place she would, like her mother, sacrifice everything for real happiness, for the closeness of belonging to someone who loved her as she loved him.

Because she wanted the Statesmen and the nobility of Luthenia to help the King, she did everything she could to make herself charming, forcing herself to overcome her natural shyness which otherwise would have left her tongue-tied.

"I am looking forward to your wedding, Ma'am," a nobleman said who she had been told owned a great deal of land and was a power in his own part of the country.

"I understand the necessity for it, as I know you do, Your Grace," Xenia answered in a low voice, "and I feel sure the King can rely on your support in the future."

The gentleman to whom she was speaking looked at her in surprise and Xenia guessed that the King had never tried to bind the influential Luthenians to him as he should have done.

She therefore moved amongst the guests deliberately seeing to it that the gentlemen should realise that she was aware of the tense and dangerous situation.

She ensured that if they had not yet thought of their own position in a possible confrontation, they should do so now.

She had no idea that it was unprecedented behaviour on the part of a Royal Personage, and though the King looked at her with surprise he did not interfere.

When finally the guests took their leave, a number of them said meaningfully to the King:

"You know Your Majesty can always count on me, and I am at your service."

As the King and Xenia, followed by his Royal relations, left the Grand Salon where they had gathered after dinner, the King said:

"What have you been saying?"

Xenia glanced at him apprehensively, not certain that he would approve.

"I thought it would be a ... good idea if those you ... entertained tonight were aware that you might ... need them ... if things are as ... serious as the Prime Minister avers."

The King did not answer for a moment, but as they reached the bottom of the stairs and Xenia was about to go to her bed-room he said:

"I am grateful. At the same time, I am astonished. I had no idea you cared for politics."

"These sort of politics," she answered, "the politics that are taking place here, will affect not only you but all your subjects."

The King was listening as she went on:

"I have a fancy that those who live outside Molnár, the great landlords, the aristocrats, have been kept in ignorance, perhaps deliberately, of what is taking place."

"That is very astute of you," the King answered. "And what you are suggesting is that I should have solicited their support before now?"

"It is never too late to begin," Xenia said with a little smile.

The Dowager Duchess joined them and there was no chance to say more.

But the King took Xenia's hand in his and kissed it.

"Thank you," he said quietly.

Then he stood and watched as she helped his aunt up the stairs.

'I hope I did the right thing,' Xenia thought.

She remembered that several times during the evening she had seen the Prime Minister look at her and his expression was unmistakably one of disapproval.

Somehow the King had to be rid of the man, but how?

79

How was it possible when apparently he had such a hold over his Cabinet and the Members of Parliament?

* * *

Having drawn the curtains, Margit came to the side of the bed.

"I have brought you the newspapers, Your Royal Highness. Perhaps you would like to glance at them while you have your breakfast? There are some very pretty sketches of your arrival."

Xenia sat up and opened the newspapers eagerly.

There were three of them and she read about herself and her arrival in one after the other.

She saw at once that the wording of the reports was almost identical in each and she was quite certain they had all been inspired from the same source.

As Margit brought back her breakfast and set it down on a table beside her, she asked:

"Are these all the newspapers that are published in Molnár?"

The elderly maid hesitated before she replied:

"There's another, Your Royal Highness."

"Then why did you not bring it?"

"I . . . it's not the type of newspaper that'd interest Your Royal Highness."

"Why not?"

Again Margit hesitated before, as if she felt she must tell the truth, she replied:

"*The People's Voice* is an independent paper that's in opposition to the Government."

"Then I would like to see it," Xenia said.

The maid looked alarmed.

"I don't think . . ." she began.

"I am sure there is one somewhere in the Palace," Xenia interrupted. "Perhaps one of the footmen would lend you a copy."

She thought Margit was about to refuse, when

80

without saying anything she went from the room.

Xenia ate her breakfast and as she finished it the maid came back.

She had hidden the newspaper under her apron and when she reached Xenia's bed-side she drew it out.

"I'll get into trouble, Your Royal Highness, if it's known that I brought you this."

"I promise I will tell no-one," Xenia said with a smile.

She opened the newspaper and realised at once why Margit was reluctant to give it to her.

Here was a very different story from the one she had read in the other newspapers.

The editorial, instead of acclaiming her arrival and the news that the marriage was to take place the following morning, denounced it in no uncertain terms, saying:

When the Romans had trouble with their conquered races they arranged a Circus to take the people's minds off their injustices and privations. The wedding of our King to the Princess Johanna of Prussen is nothing but a Luthenian Circus for which the people will have to pay whether it amuses them or not.

Xenia turned to the other pages in the paper and found many reports of oppression and injustice.

Even allowing for the hostile and aggressive tone in which such stories were written, she was quite certain that there would be some truth behind each one.

She read the newspaper from cover to cover, then she handed it back to Margit and went to have her bath.

All the time she was bathing she thought of what she had read.

At the same time, she felt helplessly that there was little or nothing she could do about it personally.

81

When she was dressing she said to Margit:

"Luthenia seems to be a prosperous country. Is there much poverty in Molnár?"

"There is nowadays, Your Royal Highness," Margit answered, "because the people get no help when they're in distress and taxes are very high. Even those who are rich can't give as generously as they used to do."

"Why are the taxes so high?" Xenia asked.

She had some idea from what she had read in the opposition newspaper, but she wanted Margit's view.

The maid did not speak for a moment, so she pleaded:

"Tell me the truth, Margit. As you know, I am a stranger here, but I want to help the King and I want to restore his popularity. Only if I understand what has gone wrong can I do anything to try and put it right."

She saw the look of surprise in the maid's eyes before she said:

"We all loved His Majesty when he was a little boy, just as we loved his lady mother for her kindness and understanding."

"I want you to love him now," Xenia said. "The newspaper I have just read speaks of great poverty, but no-one seems to care. What I am asking is, where is the money going?"

Margit looked over her shoulder almost as if she was afraid they would be overheard.

"They say, Your Royal Highness," she said cautiously, "that it's spent on buildings—a new Town Hall, great mansions for the Prime Minister and other Members of the Government, and statues, parks, and fountains in the best part of the city! People think there're too many when the schools are too few and the children who attend them are often hungry."

Xenia's lips tightened.

This was what she had read in the newspaper, but it somehow seemed worse to hear it spoken in words.

"I agree with you, Margit," she said. "It is wrong ... very wrong."

There was no time to say more because she had to hurry downstairs to drive to a Reception which was being given at the House of Parliament.

She had learnt from Count Gáspar that today there would only be a small squadron of Cavalry as an escort for the Royal Carriage.

The King was waiting for her in the Hall and she saw a faint smile on his lips as she came down wearing a gown of jonquil yellow with a little hat trimmed with small ostrich-feathers of the same colour.

Margit had arranged her hair in a most elaborate fashion, and she knew that the colour of it was enhanced not only by the yellow of her gown but also by the necklace of topaz which encircled her neck.

As it was a hot, sunny day, Margit had handed her a very small sun-shade which matched her dress, and as she and the King walked side by side through the front door and down the steps, she opened it and held it over her head.

There was a crowd outside the Palace and the women and children waved and cheered as they appeared.

There were also a number of sinister-looking men staring at them in the same glum, dissatisfied way that they had the day before.

The Cavalry with their plumed helmets looked very dashing and Xenia was sure that the cheers were more for them than for her and the King.

Today they were not alone in the carriage. Madame Gyula as her lady-in-waiting and Count Gáspar as Aide-de-Camp to the King sat facing them.

The flower-blossoming trees, the sunshine on the mountains, and the colourful skirts of the women in the streets made Xenia feel once again as if she were moving in a fairy-tale.

"When all the formalities are over," she said to the King, "I do hope I shall have a chance to see the city and also drive out into the countryside."

"I doubt if there will be enough time before we are married," the King replied.

"There must be!" Xenia exclaimed without thinking.

She was sure that Johanna would arrive before the wedding; then as far as she was concerned all this would be over and she would go back to England and obscurity.

"If it means so much to you," the King said, "we must certainly try to arrange it, although I warn you there is a very full programme ahead."

"Perhaps if we got up early and went to bed late?" Xenia suggested and he laughed.

"You must talk to the Count," he said. "He organises all our engagements for us, and he must try to shuffle them round so that you can do what you want to do."

"I will certainly do my best, Ma'am," the Count promised.

"I would not wish to refuse anything ... important," Xenia said quickly.

"It depends what you call important," the King remarked sarcastically.

Xenia did not reply and after a moment he said:

"Today we are to receive a wedding-gift from Parliament, and Kalolyi has already decided what we are to do with it."

"Can he do that?" Xenia asked.

"Who is going to stop him?" the King enquired. "What is it this time, Horváth, have you heard?"

"Nothing official, Sire," the Count replied, "but it is sure to be something that the Prime Minister thinks will add to the importance of the city."

"But only in one particular part of it," Xenia said.

She was thinking of what Margit had told her and what she had read in the newspaper.

Both the King and the Count looked at her in surprise.

"What do you mean by that?" the King asked.

Xenia was just about to reply when they entered Parliament Square and there was a burst of cheering.

Because she thought it was expected of her she turned to wave her hand and smile at the people lining the streets.

There was quite a number of them and she thought that the Prime Minister had doubtless arranged that as many people as possible should see them.

'Our arrival at the House of Parliament is of course part of the Circus,' she thought.

The crowd was thicker as they progressed through the Square, and although some of the people did not seem very enthusiastic, there were enough cheers to make Xenia hope that they were genuine.

The carriage drew up outside the front door of what was a very large and impressive building, and there was a short paved walk before Xenia and the King could reach the steps which led to the front door.

The crowds were held back by soldiers and there were also a number of policemen dressed in a uniform which Xenia thought becoming if rather ornate.

She deliberately walked slowly, feeling that it was important for those present to have time to see their King.

She realised with a little feeling of pleasure that he was responding to the cheers in a way he had not done the day before.

They had almost reached the steps when Xenia saw a banner. It was held by two women and she read:

NOBODY CARES ABOUT US!

The women looked poor, their clothes were shabby, the children with them were barefoot, and one, Xenia noticed, was on crutches.

Without saying anything to the King, she suddenly turned and walked across the grass towards the women with the banner.

It only took her a few seconds to reach them, and

the crowd round was silent in sheer astonishment as she stopped and asked:

"Tell me what your banner means? Why does nobody care about you?"

As she spoke, she realised that the Count had joined her.

"Your Royal Highness..." he began, but she held up her hand and he was silent.

"It's the children, Princess, that we're worried about," a woman answered hesitatingly.

"Why?" Xenia enquired.

The two women holding the banner had at first looked frightened because she had stopped to speak to them. Now another woman, older and obviously not so shy, interposed:

"What they're saying, Your Royal Highness, is that there's no proper Hospital. There's a small place outside the town but we've been told there's no money to keep it going and only a few children get there. When they do, the treatment's inadequate."

Xenia looked from the woman who had spoken to the women carrying the banner.

"Is that true?" she asked.

A dozen voices from the crowd which had now clustered round her answered:

"My little boy's waited for two years for glasses," one said, "and now he can see nothing!"

Xenia gathered that another child needed her tonsils removed, but there was no place where the operation could be performed. One woman had lost two children; another, three.

Now that they realised she was listening to them, more and more women came up to call out their complaints.

"Your Royal Highness, the Prime Minister will be waiting," the Count said urgently.

"I am glad you have told me this," Xenia said to the waiting women. "I promise you that both the King and I will try to help you."

She could see that the women looked incredulous, as if they thought it was very unlikely that she would be able to do anything for them. At the same time, they cheered.

Then with the Count beside her she walked back to the King, who was waiting at the foot of the steps.

Xenia looked at him apprehensively in case he was angry, but instead she thought his eyes were twinkling.

"I am sorry if what I did was wrong," she murmured as she reached his side.

"Not wrong, but certainly unprecedented," he said. "I am just waiting to hear what Kalolyi has to say about it."

There was no time to say more as they ascended the steps to where waiting for them in the doorway stood the Prime Minister.

Xenia was quite certain he had seen what had happened and she thought that he looked at her in a hostile fashion.

There was nothing, however, that he could do at the moment, because there were innumerable presentations to be made.

Then she and the King were led into a huge Hall which the Count had told her during dinner was all that was left of the old Parliament, which had been built in the sixteenth century.

It was very fine, with a great arched roof, but attached was an enormous modern building that had been erected in the last few years and had, Xenia was sure, cost an inordinate amount of money.

The Members of Parliament were all facing the platform onto which she and the King were escorted, and behind them were their wives and children, secretaries and officials, and everyone else who was connected with Parliament.

There were also the Press seated at a table near the platform. Xenia wondered if they had already been instructed what to say and given the report which would appear in their newspapers the following day.

Though the Lord Chancellor in his robes and the other dignitaries of State in theirs made an impressive sight, Xenia could see that the Prime Minister dominated them all.

As he rose and began his speech of welcome, he made it clear that it was he who had arranged the marriage that was to take place. and that it was he who had decided that a presentation should be made.

It was not only what he said, Xenia thought, it was that he was so positive and so sure of his power that he seemed to dominate the people sitting below them.

Then the moment came when he referred to the presentation.

"We decided, Your Majesty and Your Royal Highness," he said, "that as there has been so little time to choose a suitable gift, we would present you with the moneys that Parliament is prepared to spend on such an auspicious occasion."

He paused and beckoned forward the Speaker of the House, who carried an ornate casket in his hand which Xenia saw was very ancient.

He stood in front of her and the King, and the Prime Minister continued:

"The money inside this casket we present as a token of our respect and homage. We feel Your Majesty and Your Royal Highness would wish to spend it on replenishing the gold plate that is used on formal occasions and which, unfortunately, is sadly inadequate to represent the prestige and importance of our illustrious country."

The Speaker went down on one knee and held out the casket between the King and Xenia.

"You put your hand on it," the Count prompted very softly in Xenia's ear, "in acknowledgement and acceptance of the gift."

Xenia put out her gloved hand obediently and laid it beside the King's.

"I accept this gift in the spirit in which it is given," the King said.

The Speaker rose and moved away. Then, as the Prime Minister drew to one side, Xenia realised that the King was about to speak.

"May I say something first?" she asked.

If she had thrown a bomb at his feet she could not have caused more of a sensation.

The Prime Minister actually made a gesture as if he would physically stop her from speaking, but after a second's hesitation the King said:

"This is certainly a day of surprises, but of course, if that is what you wish."

As he spoke he sat down on the seat he had just vacated and Xenia was left standing alone.

She had never made a speech before and for a moment she felt as if her voice had died in her throat and her legs were so weak that they would collapse under her.

Then she told herself that whatever she did it was of no account. In a week she would be gone, and if she was to help Luthenia she must do so now or never.

"Y-your . . . Majesty . . ." she began.

Her voice was so soft that it trembled and she knew that no-one could hear her. Then, looking at the back of the Hall so that her voice would carry, she began again:

"Your Majesty, Mr. Prime Minister, Members of Parliament. I know it is unusual for a woman to speak in public, but that is perhaps why we are so often forgotten."

There was a little ripple of laughter at this and it gave Xenia confidence.

"I know," she went on, "that His Majesty is going to thank you for the generous wedding-present you have just given us, so I only wish to thank you for the welcome you have given me since I arrived in your beautiful country, and I hope you will listen to what I wish to be done with your present. If justice is done I feel I at least have a half-say in that . . ."

Again there was laughter and she continued:

"I would like it to be spent on building a Hospital for women and children, which I understand is vitally needed here in Molnár."

There was an audible gasp. Then spontaneously the wives of the Members of Parliament and all the other women who were in the building burst into applause.

Xenia smiled at them, then said quietly:

"Thank you for listening to me." And with an apologetic little smile to the King she sat down.

For a moment there was silence and Xenia glanced at the Prime Minister.

She saw the undisguised fury on his face and felt with a leap of her heart that she had now thrown down the gauntlet and there was no doubt that the battle between them had begun.

She thought he might have spoken, but the King rose.

He did not address the Prime Minister but spoke to those in the Hall.

"My mother," he began, "whom I think you all loved, always said to me that when I was married I should have to listen to my wife. I only wish she could have been here today, because I feel she would tell me not only to listen to my future wife but to obey what is obviously a wise suggestion, which I feel will meet with your approval and the approval of all the women and children in Luthenia."

He smiled and it swept the cynical look from his face.

"Who am I," he said, "a mere man, to do anything but agree whole-heartedly that this generous sum of money should be used to found a Hospital, which must, I am convinced, be called after your future Queen."

There was a burst of applause and Xenia saw with satisfaction that the reporters were scribbling away frantically in their note-books.

Then as the applause continued they began edging their way towards the entrance as if they were getting ready to rush to press and get the news out onto the streets.

Only the Prime Minister did not join in the hand-clapping but stood with narrowed eyes and grimly set lips until the King and Xenia moved to leave the building.

Then as he walked just behind them Xenia heard him say to the King:

"I do not think, Sire, for a moment that the money will be enough for the grandiose scheme which Her Royal Highness has suggested."

As he finished speaking they reached the doorway and the King turned.

"In which case, Prime Minister," he said, almost drawling the words, "some of the plans for other new buildings in the city may have to be altered, or perhaps scrapped altogether."

Without waiting for the Prime Minister's reply, the King walked down the steps with Xenia beside him.

As they drew level with the women with the banner she gave them a special wave of her hand, and she hoped that someone would tell them soon what had been said inside Parliament.

The carriage was waiting, and as Xenia and the King reached it there was a sudden scuffle in the crowd.

A number of men at the back pushed forward, shouting and booing, and as they did so a woman with a small boy who was standing in front were thrown to the ground.

The woman was not hurt, but the child, who was about four years of age, was knocked against the wheel and his leg was cut.

At the first sound of the booing the Count began trying to hurry Xenia into the carriage.

She broke away from him and knelt down beside the small boy, who was screaming while the blood was flowing down his bare leg.

She picked him up in her arms as one of the officials helped his mother to her feet.

"I'm sorry, someone pushed me," the woman was saying. "I don't want to give any trouble."

"Let me take the child, Your Royal Highness," the Count said.

"Where will you take him?" Xenia asked. "You know there is no Hospital."

The Count glanced vaguely towards the mother.

"He'll be all right," the woman said.

She was frightened at speaking to someone so grand and shaken by being thrown to the ground.

Xenia looked at her.

She was obviously very poor, although she was clean, as was the little boy she held in her arms; but her skirt was patched and her blouse had been mended in half a dozen places.

"Give me the child, Ma'am," the Count said to Xenia again.

The little boy was still crying but now he turned his head against her breast, as if he found her arms comforting.

"I think the best thing we can do," Xenia said, "is to take the injured child and his mother back to the Palace. He can be properly bandaged there, and then we can send them home."

She glanced at the King as she spoke, half-afraid that he would refuse, but now there was no doubt about the twinkle in his eyes.

"But of course!" he said. "I am sure we can squeeze in a few extra passengers."

The Count looked as if he thought the King had taken leave of his senses.

"Yes, Sire," he managed to utter after a moment.

Xenia and the King got into the carriage, Xenia still holding the small boy in her arms.

The blood was dripping from his leg onto her gown, and the King, pulling off his gloves, produced a handkerchief and tied it neatly round the wound.

The mother, dazed, and speechless from what was happening to her, sat opposite Xenia, while Madame Gyula was squeezed against the Count and would have liked to protest at the indignity but she was too afraid to do so in front of the King.

They set off.

The boos and shouts had died away as soon as the accident happened and now there were only cheers as the carriage drove back the way it had come.

The people in the Square stared incredulously at Xenia holding a child in her arms and with even more astonishment at the ragged woman sitting opposite her.

She could see them asking one another what had happened and who the strangers in the Royal Carriage were.

But by the time they reached the Palace it seemed as if the news, if not of the child's accident, then certainly of what had been said in Parliament, had preceded them.

Now there was no doubt of the sincerity of the cheers that greeted them outside the gold-tipped railings.

It was impossible for Xenia to wave but she smiled and bowed her head and the King waved in the manner she thought he should have done when she first arrived in Molnár.

Only when they reached the steps leading into the Palace did Xenia hand the little boy to his mother and say to the Count:

"I think they should be taken to the Housekeeper's room to have the leg attended to, then both of them should be given a good meal."

"I will see to it, Ma'am," the Count replied, and he remained in the carriage when it drove away to a side door.

As Xenia walked up the steps with the King she looked with some concern at the stains of blood on her yellow gown.

The King must have been thinking the same thing, for he said:

"I will buy you another, and we ought to put that

93

gown in a glass case and label it 'The first shot of de-
fiance against Kalolyi'!"

"The Prime Minister was very angry," Xenia said.

"There will be nothing he can do," the King said
positively. "The news will be all over Molnár today
and Luthenia tomorrow."

They reached the Hall and when Xenia would
have gone upstairs to change her gown the King put
his hand under her arm and drew her into a small
Salon.

He shut the door behind them and as she looked
at him, waiting to hear what he had to say, he said:

"I suppose you know that you have started a
revolution of your own? I am not quite certain what
the outcome will be."

He spoke gravely but there was a smile in his
eyes she had not seen before.

She did not reply and he stood looking at her
before he said:

"What has happened? Why are you changed?
Why are you so different from what you were three
months ago?"

"Perhaps I have ... grown older and ... wiser,"
Xenia said lightly.

"I do not understand," the King said, as if he
was puzzling it out for himself.

"Do not let us worry about me," Xenia said. "It
is you we are concerned with."

She gave a little sigh.

"I was so afraid you would be angry."

"You—afraid?" the King questioned.

"I know it was a big step to defy the Prime
Minister publicly, but I have a feeling the only way
we can beat him is by arousing public opinion
against him."

"You realise he will never forgive you," the King
said.

"It does not matter. It is you who are important."

The King walked away from her towards one of
the windows that overlooked the garden.

"Suppose that after all this I fail you?" he asked.
"It was a very courageous thing for you to have done.
What I am wondering is if I can carry on where you
have begun."

"Of course you can!" Xenia answered. "You just
have to think of ways by which the population
will become aware that what they are suffering is the
Prime Minister's doing . . . not yours."

"He has made it very clear in the past," the King
said, "that I am responsible for the decrees that go
out in my name, and the taxes."

"Then you must stop it."

"How? How?" he asked. "It is not going to be
easy."

"We have had luck so far," Xenia said. "If I had
not spoken to those women with the banner, if they
had not been there, I would not have found out about
the Hospital."

"It never struck me until now that there is not
one."

"The Prime Minister, however, will say there is
one. But it is outside the town and very inadequate
for what is needed. Besides, I can understand how
the women would hate for a child to be taken a long
way from them. And if they have other children,
how can they go to see the one who is ill if the hospital is far from Molnár?"

"You are right—of course you are right!" the King
said. "But I do not mind betting that somehow Kalolyi will divert the money for the Hospital to the things
on which he has set his heart."

"Then you must find it by other means," Xenia
said. "Ask the great landowners to contribute, and if
you cannot get it that way, then threaten to sell the
Crown Jewels!"

She spoke positively and the King threw back
his head and laughed.

"You are magnificent!" he exclaimed. "When
I listen to you I find that Kalolyi is sinking into his
proper perspective."

"He is only an ambitious upstart," Xenia replied, "who has grown to power because you have let him."

"I thought it would be my fault sooner or later," the King said.

"Of course it is!" Xenia agreed. "You have your health and strength, and you have brains, if you want to use them. What are you waiting for?"

Again she spoke without thinking, and now the King laughed so much that he sat down in an arm-chair to go on laughing.

"You are incorrigible!" he cried. "Why did I not realise before that you were like this? With you beside me I shall be ruling not only Luthenia but half of Europe as well!"

"Why not?" Xenia asked. "Do you realise how important you are at this particular moment in history?"

"Important?" the King queried.

"Mr. Donington told me that Great Britain will support you in anything you do."

"Who is Mr. Donington?"

"An official of the British Foreign Office who escorted me to Vienna."

"Why did he say that? Did you question him?"

"Of course I did!" Xenia answered. "I wanted to know why I had to come here in such a hurry, and he said that Great Britain was aware of the unrest in Luthenia and that you were of vital importance to the balance of power."

"Why the hell has no-one told me this before?" the King asked irritably.

"I suppose they were too afraid, or perhaps they thought you would not listen."

"That is true," the King admitted. "The British Minister in Molnár is a bore, so I never thought of having a private conversation with him. Or perhaps Kalolyi has deliberately contrived that I should never have a chance of being alone with any of the Foreign Ministers."

"Then why do you not invite them to the Palace, one by one?" Xenia suggested.

The King rose to his feet.

"That is something I will do immediately after we are married," he said. "By that time I imagine you will have hundreds more suggestions, or rather I should say 'instructions' for me to carry out!"

Xenia did not answer.

Instead, she thought that she had only a few more days with him, and the idea was so depressing that it was almost a physical pain.

* * *

After a quiet luncheon with the King's relatives and Madame Gyula and the Count, Xenia remembered that the Prime Minister had said there was to be a Press Conference.

She was just about to ask the Count when it was to take place when an Aide-de-Camp came into the room to say:

"I thought you would wish to know, Your Majesty, that the representatives of the Press are here, but a messenger has come from the Prime Minister to say he thinks in the circumstances it would be a mistake for either Your Majesty or Her Royal Highness to see them."

"Has he given any reason for this change of plan?" Xenia asked.

"I understand, Your Royal Highness, that the Prime Minister thinks that some of the questions may prove too impertinent or too embarrassing for you to answer."

Xenia looked at the King.

"Shall I reply?" she asked.

"Of course," he answered. "If you remember, the Prime Minister said he was sure they would wish to know intimate details of yourself and your trousseau."

"Will you inform the messenger," she said to the Aide-de-Camp, "that I am perfectly prepared to answer any questions from the representatives of the Press, and I am sure that His Majesty will join me later in case they have anything they wish to ask of him."

The Aide-de-Camp would have bowed and left the room, but as he reached the door Xenia asked:

"Is there a reporter from *The People's Voice* present?"

The Aide-de-Camp repeated almost stupidly:

"*Th-The People's Voice?*"

"That is a paper which is against the Government," the Count said.

Again Xenia looked at the King.

As if he realised exactly what she was doing, he said:

"I think on such an important occasion as a Royal Wedding every newspaper should be included in the Press Conference."

"Do you mean that, Sire?" the Count asked. "*The People's Voice* has been violently anti-Monarchy for some time."

"What they invent would doubtless be far more harmful than anything they will hear from us," the King replied.

"I will send for a reporter, Sire," the Count said, "and ask the other representatives to wait in patience until he arrives."

"What is all this about?" the Dowager Duchess of Mildenburg enquired, who had been listening to what was being said. "When I was young the newspaper reporters were treated like pariahs, but nowadays I am told they are encouraged even by Queen Victoria!"

"We have to move with the times, Aunt Elizabeth," the King said, "and the more the people can read, the more they are capable of voting for the right representatives in Parliament."

"I am sure you are right, dearest István," the Dowager Duchess replied, "and yet it seems to me a very revolutionary step that you and dear Johanna should actually receive such people."

"They are quite ordinary flesh and blood," the King said with a smile.

"Your grandfather would certainly not have thought so."

The King laughed.

"Johanna is convinced that they are more valuable to us than a Regiment of soldiers, and I am not certain she is not right."

He smiled at Xenia as he spoke, and then he said unexpectedly:

"We have a little time on our hands. What would you like to do?"

"See the Palace," Xenia said quickly, "especially the pictures."

"Come along then," the King said. "It will take the best part of an hour to collect this anarchist you insist on including in your cosy chat, so let us play truant for as long as we can."

He held out his hand and she put hers into it, and leading her as if she were a child he set off with her to explore the Palace.

It was even more fascinating than Xenia had expected, and she found that the King was very knowledgeable about his possessions, especially the paintings.

"I never thought, I never dreamt, that I should see anything so beautiful," she enthused over several Canalettos.

"One day I will take you to Vienna," the King said. "That is, if we are left with any money which has not been spent on your good works."

His words gave her an idea.

"Are you rich?" she asked.

"It depends what you want to buy," he answered.

"I was thinking," she said, "that if we started a fund to help the poorest people in the city and contributed towards a Hospital and other things that are desperately needed, we would encourage other people to give, especially if you call it 'The King's Fund.'"

"It is certainly an idea," the King agreed.

"If you cannot afford it," Xenia said tentatively, "I suppose it would be possible to get a very high price in Paris or London for pictures like these."

"If you are going to sack the Palace," the King said positively, "then I am not going to listen to you."

"You have to consider whether you would be better off less a few pictures or the Palace itself," Xenia snapped without choosing her words.

There was silence, then she said quickly:

"I am ... sorry. I should not have spoken like that, but there is so much to be done and so very little time to do it."

"Do you really believe the revolutionaries are knocking on the door?" the King asked.

She could not say that as far as she was concerned time was of urgent importance.

Every breath she drew meant that she was a second nearer to the moment when like Cinderella her glamour would be stripped away from her and she would be on the train back to England.

"If it is so urgent for us to be married," she managed to say after a moment, "then I am not exaggerating when I say that any step you wish to take to avert a revolution should be taken at once."

"You are right," the King agreed. "At the same time, it is hard to believe I can be swept away as easily as that."

"I think we have to be fair and say that the Prime Minister will do everything he can to avert it," Xenia said, "but on his own terms and in his own way."

"Blast him!" the King swore. "If he had not been so overbearing, this dissatisfaction would never have built up in the first place."

"But it is there now," Xenia said, "and it is something we have to face."

They were speaking in the Picture-Gallery, and now the Count approached them.

"The Editor from *The People's Voice* has come

himself, Ma'am," he said to Xenia, "and judging from the expression on his face, I think you may be in for some pretty tough cross-questioning."

"I am not afraid," Xenia answered.

Once again she put her hand into the King's.

"Come and support me," she said. "I have a feeling that no-one is going to mention my trousseau or even ask me what is my favourite pudding! It is going to be politics . . . politics all the way!"

"And I am quite certain," the King said dryly, "they will prove extremely indigestible!"

Chapter Five

Galloping beside the King, Xenia thought she had never been so happy in her whole life.

For the first time she was riding a horse of the type her mother had described to her so often, a thoroughbred which was spirited and at the same time responded to every touch of her hand.

The snow on the peaks of the mountains was brilliant against a clear blue sky and the grass over which they were riding on the Steppes was filled with wild flowers.

It was so lovely, so colourful, that Xenia felt there was no artist living who could do it justice.

It was also an indescribable joy to be alone with the King.

They had in fact a mounted escort, but the four troopers who accompanied them kept in the background and it was easy for Xenia to forget their very existence.

In the last few days it had been almost impossible for her to be alone with the King, for there had been so many things to do.

After the accident to the small boy after they had left the House of Parliament, they had gone on Xenia's suggestion to call at his home and enquire as to his health.

It was an excuse which made it possible for the

King to see a part of the city he had never visited before.

As they drove through the narrow, dirty streets hidden behind the facade of impressive buildings erected by the Prime Minister, she knew he was shocked and appalled.

There were houses which looked as if they were on the verge of falling down, there were open drains, and there was also, they found on enquiry, a scarcity of pumps from which the people could draw water.

The mother of the little boy they had befriended lived in one room of a dilapidated house in which thirty other people lived, and existed on what Xenia felt must be the borderline of starvation.

They left some presents and money, and when they drove back to the Palace she thought there was a new expression of determination about the King that had not been there before.

He had announced to the Press the previous day that he intended setting up a "King's Fund" and would use the money to alleviate distress and to improve housing conditions.

Afterwards Xenia had laughed at the expression on the faces of the newspaper reporters as he spoke.

"They goggled at you like gold-fish!" she said. "I thought their eyes would fall out of their sockets!"

"It is sad that they never got round to talking about your trousseau!" the King teased.

This was not surprising, for, as they had expected, the Editor of *The People's Voice* bombarded the King with questions and was obviously not interested in the feminine point of view.

The newspapers, even the conventional Government-inspired ones, carried headlines which Xenia knew would infuriate the Prime Minister.

THE PRINCESS WHO CARES they had shouted in bold capitals after she had befriended the little boy.

THE KING INTENDS TO GET THINGS MOVING! was the headline the following day.

It was all very exciting and Xenia longed to have

time alone with the King to discuss everything that
had happened.

But the Palace was filling up for the wedding with
relatives who lived nearby and every day brought
answers to invitations from the Monarchs of neigh-
bouring States.

Everyone expected to stay in the Palace, and
there was a continual shuffling of places and changing of accommodations when a guest who was more
important than others had to be moved in, which
meant that someone else had to be moved out.

The Prime Minister, moreover, was determined
after their visit to the poor quarters of the city that
they should not uncover any more horrors.

He therefore arranged for the King and Xenia to
visit other towns in the country and away from Molnár.

This involved leaving early in the Royal Train,
being greeted by crowds on arrival, inspecting a
Guard of Honour, meeting civic dignitaries, and usu-
ally having a long-drawn-out luncheon, at which
there seemed to be interminable speeches.

It was impossible to refuse to make these visits,
as the King would have liked to do. But once the
Prime Minister had told the Mayor and Corporation
to expect the Royal Couple, Xenia felt that it was
worthwhile. The cheers which had seemed perfunc-
tory on arrival were on their departure effusive and
sincere.

Now there was only one more day before the
wedding, and she expected Johanna to arrive at any
moment.

She had therefore bullied Count Gáspar into al-
tering their programme so that she and the King
could ride together and be "off duty" at least for the
best part of the last day.

"You will have plenty of time to ride on your
honeymoon," Ma'am," Count Gáspar suggested.

"I need the exercise now," Xenia replied.

The Count laughed.

"You are indefatigable, Ma'am. Most women who look as frail and ethereal as you do would have collapsed long ago from the strenuousness of the last few days."

Xenia did not reply. Although some nights she had been very tired, she was enjoying herself and there was no question of her collapsing.

Every moment had a fascination of its own because she was seeing things she had never seen before but which she had heard about from her mother.

She admitted to herself that every detail was enhanced because she was fighting for the King and because they were united in a battle which drew them secretly and closely together.

When the King heard that they were going riding he said to the Count:

"If we are really to play truant, I intend to take Her Royal Highness to see the Sacred Falls."

"What are they?" Xenia asked. "I do not seem to have heard of them before."

"They belong to the very early history of Luthenia," the King replied, "when the people treated them as a kind of Oracle."

"It sounds exciting!" Xenia exclaimed.

"They may not really be very sacred," the King said, "but they are extremely beautiful."

"Then of course I am longing to see them," Xenia answered.

She found amongst Johanna's clothes several very attractive, exceedingly well-cut riding-habits.

It was not difficult to choose which she would wear as the weather was very warm and she knew it would be exceedingly hot at midday.

She therefore let Margit dress her in a habit of white piqué, a material which had first been introduced in Paris by the ladies who rode in the Bois.

It was decorated with emerald-green braid and Xenia found that there were little short boots of green leather and gloves to match.

Her small hat was decorated with a gauze veil

of the same green, and the King thought as they rode away from the Palace that her eyes were shining like two emeralds.

Now as they steadied their horses from a gallop into a trot, Xenia looked over her shoulder at the King and said:

"That is better! I did not realise until now how constrained and tense I have been feeling."

"We have left all the dragons behind," the King replied, "and I must say the air smells better without them."

The fragrance of the wild flowers was in fact almost overwhelming, and Xenia, looking at the beauty of the mountains, said:

"Would it not be wonderful if we could ride away to the farthest horizon and never have to come back?"

"And how soon do you think you would be bored?" the King asked mockingly.

"I should be asking you that question," Xenia retorted.

She thought as she spoke that the cynicism and the aloof indifference or boredom which she had seen on his face on her arrival had almost vanished.

He was alert, and ever since they had been fighting the Prime Minister, he had had the air of a man who, goaded into battle, was determined to be the victor.

"I have a Castle in the mountains," the King said unexpectedly, "but somehow I never thought that you would enjoy the simple life."

"I would love to stay in the mountains," Xenia answered.

As she spoke she knew that she would never have the chance of seeing the King's Castle or even the mountains themselves, except from a distance.

'To me they are out of reach,' she thought, and knew that her "midnight" was very near, ushered in by Johanna's arrival.

'She will come tomorrow,' Xenia told herself silently.

Because the thought of leaving Luthenia was like a physical pain, she was afraid the King would realise what she was suffering and so she touched her horse with her spur.

Again she was galloping with the tireless, rhythmic stride that was characteristic of a Hungarian-bred horse. The King was beside her and there was an exhilaration about moving so swiftly, the soft, cool air against her face.

They had ridden for two hours when the King said:

"We are nearing the Falls and we must allow our escort to catch up with us so that they can hold our horses."

Xenia drew in her reins and as she did so she said:

"You ride magnificently! I knew you would."

"That is a compliment I can return whole-heartedly," the King replied. "In fact I had no idea that you were such an outstanding horsewoman."

"I have not ridden for a long time," Xenia said.

She realised she had spoken without thinking, and added quickly:

"At least, it seems a long time. It always does when I am not in the saddle."

"As soon as we are married we will ride every day," the King said. "I have some excellent horses at the Summer Palace which I want to show you."

"I long to see them," Xenia answered, and tried to prevent her voice from recording not enthusiasm but despair in knowing that this was something she would never do.

The King drew his horse a little closer to hers before he said in a tone of voice she had not heard before from him:

"Every day since you have come to Molnár you have looked more lovely than the last. I thought

107

you were beautiful three months ago when I came to Slovia, and I had not seen you since you were grown up, but now you look different."

"In what way?" Xenia asked.

She knew she should change the conversation and not let him talk about her, but she was curious.

Besides, too, because he was paying her compliments she felt a strange sensation within her, a feeling she did not recognise, and yet it seemed to take possession of her.

The King was looking at her face as if he was considering his words.

"There is something very young about you," he said reflectively, "and yet in many things you are very old, and so clever that I am astounded at how much you know and how adept you are at handling people."

"You are . . . flattering me!" Xenia said shyly.

"And you are also," the King went on as if she had not spoken, "so lovely that I am finding it hard to wait until the day after tomorrow before I tell you how much you mean to me."

Xenia drew in her breath in surprise, then her eyes met the King's and it was impossible to look away.

"I want to kiss you," he said in a low voice. "I want it more than I have ever wanted anything in my whole life!"

There was a throb of passion behind the words, which made Xenia feel as if her heart turned over in her breast.

Then as she still stared at him, unable to move, she heard the approach of their body-guard.

With the soldiers behind them, the King led the way up the side of the mountain.

They climbed in single-file until halfway up among the thick foliage of the trees he drew his horse to a standstill.

"We have to walk from here," he said to Xenia.

The soldiers went to their horses' heads, but before Xenia could slip to the ground the King lifted her from the saddle.

Feeling his hands on her waist and the closeness of his body made her feel again the strange sensation that seemed to ripple through her.

Then she was free and he led the way along a small path that was really no more than a sheep-track winding between the tree-trunks.

They walked for quite some way before Xenia heard the sound of falling water, and a moment later they emerged into the open and in front of them were the Sacred Falls.

They started high up the mountain and fell hundreds of feet down into a narrow valley to form a stream between two perpendicular cliffs.

The rocks on either side of the Falls were covered with wild flowers, and the silver water reflecting the sunshine and the vivid blue of the sky made the most beautiful picture Xenia had ever seen.

"Do you want to go behind the water?" the King asked as she looked without speaking.

"Behind?" she questioned.

"It is where in ancient times the priests went to listen to the Oracle," he explained. "When the Falls were quiet and gentle in the summer, as they are now, they imagined that the gods who lived high on the mountains were pleased with them. But in the winter when the water rushed down in a torrent from the snows, they thought the gods were angry."

"I can understand how much it meant to them," Xenia said, "for I have never seen anything so beautiful."

"Let us consult the Oracle," the King suggested. "We will ask it if we are to be successful and perhaps we shall get the right answer."

"I hope so ... I pray so," Xenia said seriously.

She knew the King was looking at her, but because she was shy she would not meet his eyes again.

She was in fact pulsatingly conscious of what he had said when they were waiting for the soldiers.

"Follow me," he said now, and they started to climb a short distance down between the rocks until they reached the falling water.

When they were close to it Xenia could see that there was a path leading behind the Falls and this was passable without getting wet because the rocks above jutted out.

"You must be careful. This path is slippery," the King said. "I would not wish you to end up in the pool below, for I am told the bodies sacrificed by the priests never came to the surface, which meant they were accepted by the gods."

"The bodies?" Xenia questioned.

The King smiled.

"Naturally they made sacrifices. It is part of every primitive religion, and I fancy a pure Athenian maiden was the victim."

"I do not like to think about it," Xenia said.

"Then give me your hand and move carefully," the King said with a smile.

Obediently Xenia put her hand into his, and because they had both removed their gloves the touch of his fingers gave her a sudden thrill that was like a shaft of sunlight moving through her body.

'This is love!' she thought, and knew with a feeling of combined rapture and consternation that she loved the King!

She had in fact loved him for a long time, but she had been afraid to admit it to herself.

Now there was no mistaking her feelings and instinctively her fingers tightened on his.

"It is all right," he said reassuringly. "It is safer than it looks once we are inside."

It was in fact only the entrance that was narrow and dangerous.

Inside there was a cave behind the Falls and the ground was dry except within a few inches of the Falls itself.

The water fell like a silver veil, and because, as the King had said, it was summer, instead of the

110

deafening roar which must have been made by a winter torrent, there was only a soft sound, almost like music.

The sunlight turned every drop of water into a minute rainbow which sparkled dazzlingly, giving Xenia the feeling that she was in an Aladdin's Cave of magical jewels that glittered with a light of their own.

Without releasing her hand the King drew her back a little way into the cave.

"I have something to tell you," he said. "I have not had a chance so far this morning."

"What is it?" she asked.

"Do you remember telling me that one of the reasons for so much dissatisfaction amongst the men of the city was that the Luthenian beer was heavily taxed so they were forced to buy Austrian ale which was cheaper but which they did not like?"

Margit had told Xenia this and she had repeated it to the King, suggesting that he should insist on the tax being lifted from the Luthenian beer so that the local Brewers could start working again.

"I thought over what you said," the King went on, "and considered it so strange that I sent someone I trust to investigate the imports which come from Austria."

"What did you find?"

"I found that Kalolyi is part-owner of the Austrian Brewery which supplies Luthenia with beer!"

Xenia stared at him.

"Part-owner? But that is disgraceful! He is benefitting himself by taxing his own countrymen."

"Exactly!" the King said. "And I am now quite certain that he is defrauding the citizens of Luthenia in other ways also."

Xenia gave a little cry of delight.

"Now you can get rid of him!" she exclaimed.

"Not so easily!" a voice said.

Both Xenia and the King started.

Then from the opposite side of the Falls from

which they had entered came the Prime Minister, and, incredible though it seemed to Xenia, he was holding a pistol in his hand.

"What are you doing here?" the King enquired.

"When I learnt early this morning of your destination," the Prime Minister replied, "I found you had played right into my hands."

"What do you mean by that?"

"It is very simple," the Prime Minister answered. "When I learnt that you were making enquiries about me I knew it was a case, Your Majesty, of either you or me."

He spoke in a manner which made Xenia feel as if a cold hand clutched her heart, and a suspicion of his intentions confronted her menacingly like a venomous snake.

The King released her hand and she put it protectively against her breast.

"Are you threatening me, Kalolyi?" the King asked calmly.

"It is not a question of a threat, Your Majesty," the Prime Minister replied. "I am simply informing you that you and Her Royal Highness will not return from this expedition to the Sacred Falls!"

There was something so evil in his voice that involuntarily Xenia cried:

"No . . . no!"

"It is just two steps forward for each of you," the Prime Minister went on, "or, if you prefer, I can shoot you first. The sound will not be heard above the noise of the water."

"You appear to have thought this all out very carefully," the King said, still speaking in the even tones he had used before.

He was showing no fear of the man confronting him, Xenia thought with a feeling of pride.

Instead, he seemed to be standing almost at his ease, one hand in his pocket, the other loose and relaxed at his side.

112

But she knew that they were both in deadly danger and she could only hope wildly that if she had to die she would do so with dignity and without screaming.

"You should know by now, Your Majesty, that I am a very resourceful man," the Prime Minister said. "I have in fact already arranged that if Your Majesty should suffer a regrettable accident or be unable to rule the country in the traditional manner, Luthenia will become a State of the Austrian Empire, under my administration."

"So you are a traitor amongst other things!" the King said accusingly.

"It is a common-sense solution," the Prime Minister answered. "But if you had not interfered, there would have been no reason for me to resort to such extreme methods."

He paused. Then, looking at Xenia, he said:

"Perhaps the person most to blame is Her Royal Highness. Women are at the root of most trouble, and this is no exception."

"You will leave Her Royal Highness out of this," the King said. "And I am prepared to bargain with you—my life for hers."

The Prime Minister smiled unpleasantly.

"You can hardly imagine I should be so foolish as to leave alive a witness of your untimely death?"

The King did not answer and the Prime Minister went on:

"But we must waste no more time. I must return to Molnár to await the reports of those who accompanied you that you have vanished without trace and they can only imagine that the gods of the Sacred Falls have accepted a Royal sacrifice for the good of Luthenia."

He was jeering at them, Xenia knew, and at the same time enjoying himself and the power that his position gave him.

"What I suggest," he said almost briskly, "is that

you, Your Royal Highness, take the ladies' privilege of going first."

Xenia looked at him but she could not speak. Her voice had died in her throat.

"Just two steps forward," the Prime Minister said. "I promise you you will not suffer after the first moment of terror, and no-one has ever returned from the bottom of the Falls to relate what their feelings were."

Xenia felt as if she had turned to stone.

The pistol in the Prime Minister's hand was still pointed at the King.

She knew that he would not hesitate to use it on both of them and then throw their bodies over the edge and return to Molnár.

No-one would ever know what had happened or that the Prime Minister had been present.

It was a brilliant plot, she thought, and she and the King had walked into it without having any idea what desperate methods the Prime Minister would employ to save himself from exposure.

It flashed through her mind that if she had to die she would at least be dying with the King, and because she loved him that in itself was a comfort, but a very small one.

"Take the first step, Your Royal Highness!" the Prime Minister said commandingly.

Xenia felt as if her feet were clamped to the ground and any movement was impossible.

Then as she looked despairingly at the King, wanting to say good-bye, wanting to tell him how much she loved him, he drew his hand from his pocket.

There was a sudden tinkle as a number of gold coins, glittering in the light from the water, fell to the ground.

Xenia glanced down to see what had happened and the Prime Minister did the same.

In that split second of inattention the King sprang

forward and forced the Prime Minister's arm up in the air.

He must have pulled the trigger, for the shot vibrated round the cave; then the two men were struggling, both of them fighting for their lives.

One moment they were grappling together, the next minute the Prime Minister's body was silhouetted against the water, his arms outstretched, his feet without any substance beneath them, and with a shrill scream he disappeared.

It all happened so swiftly that it was hard to believe that the whole episode had not been a figment of the imagination.

Then Xenia gave a little murmur of horror and turned towards the King.

She felt his arms go round her, holding her tight, giving her a sense of security that superseded the terror of what she had seen.

Then as she raised her white, frightened face to his, his mouth came down on hers.

For a moment his lips were hard and hurt her, until as he felt the softness of hers and knew she was trembling his kiss became more gentle, and yet insistent and compelling.

It was then that the sensations she had felt before seemed to rise in Xenia to sweep away everything but the realisation that she was being kissed and that she loved the King.

She knew this was what she had wanted and longed for all her life when she had sought the same love that her father and mother had known.

This was love so overwhelming that everything else receded into the distance and she could think only of the King and the closeness of him and the feelings his lips evoked within her.

With the water singing beside them and in the dim light of the cave they were in an enchanted place that belonged not to the world but to the gods who had made it sacred.

After time had passed—it might have been a minute, an hour, even a century—the King raised his head.

He looked down at her and because she could not help it she whispered:

"I love ... you! I love ... you!"

"And I love you, my brave darling!" the King replied.

Then he was kissing her again, kissing her wildly and passionately, as if he must express his relief that they were still alive and free of the evil which had menaced them.

He kissed her eyes, her cheeks, her ears, and the softness of her neck.

He put up his hand to pull her hat from her head so that he could touch the shining glory of her hair, and she felt that her whole body melted into his and they were one person, each indivisible from the other.

Finally the King raised his head again to say gently:

"We are free, my precious one, and alive!"

Xenia hid her face against his shoulder.

"I thought ... we must ... die," she whispered.

"I thought so too," the King admitted. "How could I have known—how could I have guessed—that he was a murderer at heart?"

"I knew he was ... horrible and ... evil the first time I ... touched his hand," Xenia murmured.

The King straightened his shoulders.

"The world will be a better place without him," he said. "But you realise, my darling, that no-one, and I mean no-one, must ever know how he died. We must never speak of this again, in case someone should overhear, as he overheard what we were saying."

"What will ... happen when he ... does not ... return?" Xenia asked.

"There will be a great deal of speculation," the King replied, "but since Kalolyi is sure to have covered his tracks cleverly, we will not be involved."

He kissed Xenia again, then he said:

"Come—let us go home. I think you have been through enough for one day."

He took her by the hand and led her very carefully from the cave back along the ledge and out into the sunshine.

Xenia found it impossible to look down at the water splashing over the rocks at the bottom of the Falls.

As if he understood without words what she was feeling, the King drew her up the path until they reached the trees.

"Do not look back, my darling," he said, "and remember, nothing has happened except that you have seen the Sacred Falls and thought them very beautiful."

He looked at Xenia and added:

"And I have no words to tell you how beautiful you are and how much I love you!"

His words brought the sunlight into Xenia's eyes.

"How could I ever have dreamt that I would feel like this?" the King asked.

He bent his head and as if he could not help himself he kissed her lips.

Then resolutely, knowing it was imperative that they return home, he led her back through the forest.

They rode quickly and in silence and only as they arrived back at the Palace did Xenia feel suddenly weak, and the whole horror of what had occurred swept over her.

"I want you to go and rest," the King said as he lifted her from the saddle of her horse. "I will explain to everybody that you are tired after such a long ride, and whatever engagements are planned for this afternoon I will fulfill them without you."

"No . . . I . . . I shall be . . . all right . . ." Xenia began.

"What I am giving you is an order," the King said. "You wanted me to be authoritative, and I am starting on you!"

She smiled because she knew how much meaning there was behind the words. Then, after Margit had helped her into bed, she knew she was in fact exhausted and wanted only to sleep.

* * *

She slept for some hours and awoke to find that the afternoon was drawing to a close.

She wondered what the King was doing and if already people in the city were wondering what had become of the Prime Minister.

She was curious to the point where she wanted to get up and find out what was happening.

But she knew it would be a tremendous effort to move and realised that one of the reasons was that she was stiff from riding after she had not been on a horse for so long.

It had been an inexpressible pleasure at the time, but now physically she was paying the price.

"I want to see the King," she told herself, and fell asleep again, feeling as if his lips were on hers.

* * *

The following morning Margit called her as usual with the newspapers, and now *The People's Voice* was automatically included with the other three.

Xenia sat up in bed to scan the headlines, thinking that there might be something about the disappearance of the Prime Minister, although she thought it unlikely.

Instead there were headlines in enormous print about the King's speech the previous day.

Xenia remembered that she should have been present at a Civic Reception at which they would receive presents from the Mayor and Corporation of Molnár.

It was disappointing to find that she had missed what she knew must have been a sensational declaration by the King.

He had told the city dignitaries that he had, be-

118

fore the Reception, instructed the Chancellor of the Exchequer to reduce all taxes, especially those relating to industry.

He continued by saying that in the future he intended to see that those who wished to start up new industries in Luthenia or to enlarge existing ones would be able to obtain special Government grants.

Xenia smiled as she could imagine the surprise on the faces of those who listened to him and the excitement of the reporters.

This was just what she had hoped he would say, and she knew the fact that there would no longer be any opposition from a Parliament that had lost their leader had given an added emphasis to his plans.

"This is good news, Your Royal Highness!" Margit said with a smile.

"Very good!" Xenia agreed. "And now, Margit, what have I to do this morning?"

"Today there are many deputations to be received by Your Royal Highness and to present their gifts," Margit answered. "The first is at ten-thirty A.M."

Xenia realised she had very little time and hastily ate her breakfast and had her bath.

When she went downstairs she knew that what she wanted more than anything else was to see the King, but she was kept busy until luncheon-time.

Then, because it was a large luncheon-party with all his relatives and the other guests who had arrived for the wedding, they were seated at opposite ends of the table.

Nevertheless, when they met in the Salon before luncheon he had raised her hands to his lips, and as she felt a little thrill run through her because he was touching her she knew he felt the same.

In the afternoon the King had a meeting with the Privy Council, at which, in the Prime Minister's absence, he put forward a large number of suggestions and instructions which left those who listened impressed and at the same time apprehensive.

He was well aware that they were wondering

what the Prime Minister would say on his return and
how they might find themselves "between the devil
and the deep blue sea."

By the evening a strange rumour began to circu-
late through the city.

It was said that the Prime Minister had disappeared because there might be charges brought
against him for illicit trading with a foreign country
and for intriguing with Austria against the indepen-
dence of Luthenia.

Nobody knew from where such stories originated,
but they continued to be repeated from the highest
citizen to the lowest.

As Xenia dressed for dinner she felt despairingly
that this would be her last evening with the King,
and as far as she could see there was no chance of
being alone with him.

She was quite convinced that before she drove to
the Cathedral tomorrow morning Johanna would appear to take her place.

She was running it fine, but Xenia had calculated
that if she had learnt on the first or second day after
her arrival in Molnár of the early date of the King's
marriage she could have arrived by yesterday evening or, allowing for train delays, by today.

"She will come this afternoon," Xenia told herself.

She knew that somehow she must kiss the King
once more because it was all she would have to remember in the future.

As Margit fastened a diamond necklace round her
neck and attached several diamond stars in her
hair, she told herself that this was the last time she
would ever wear jewels.

She knew now that she would never be married
and her life would be one of empty loneliness.

It would be impossible for her to love any other
man as she loved the King; for, as her mother had
done before her, she had given him not only her
heart but also her soul and her mind.

"And I have saved him!" she told herself.

It was some consolation that she had preserved his throne and he was in fact a very different man from the bitter, cynical Monarch who had met her when she arrived.

She went down the stairs to the Salon, and to-night there was no formality, so the guests did not assemble before the King to be presented.

Instead, they all mingled together and there was the chatter of voices and the sound of laughter as Xenia entered.

One glance told her that the King was not there and it was in fact twenty minutes later before he appeared, full of apologies.

"I thought perhaps, István, you were having a bachelor-dinner on your last night of freedom," one of his relations said jokingly.

"I am a very willing prisoner of the bonds of matrimony," the King replied, and his eyes met Xenia's as he spoke.

Then they trooped into the Dining-Room and once again Xenia was not beside him, but had another Monarch and an elderly relative on either side of her.

After dinner the ladies withdrew to the Salon and Xenia waited impatiently for the King to join them.

"I must see him alone ... I must!" she said to herself.

Every time the door opened she thought it would be a servant coming to tell her that someone was asking for her urgently and when she investigated she would find Johanna.

The King entered the Salon, laughed and talked with his guests for a short while, then came to her side.

"I have something to tell you," he said in a low voice.

She looked into his eyes and everyone else seemed to vanish from her sight.

She was sure he felt the same as he drew her

out of the room through one of the windows that opened onto the garden.

They walked across the lawn as the last rays of the sun were playing on the fountain.

"What is it?" she asked.

"I have this afternoon appointed a Deputy Prime Minister until such time as we can hold a General Election."

"Was it safe for you to do that?" she asked quickly.

"The rumours as to the Prime Minister's disappearance were so disturbing that I felt justified in taking such a step."

"Oh, I am glad, so very glad!" Xenia cried. "Now everyone will realise that you are in control and no-one else."

"That is exactly what I felt," the King smiled, "and I knew you would understand."

They stopped at the end of the garden and were out of sight of the Palace.

"I have not had a chance," the King said quietly, "to tell you how much I owe you. I am well aware that none of this would have happened if it had not been for you."

"Now you are everything I would want you to be," Xenia said.

"You have inspired and guided me," the King went on, "and tomorrow I shall be able to tell you not only how grateful I am but also how much I love you!"

He drew her into his arms and kissed her until she felt the garden swing round her and he carried her into the glory of the setting sun.

There was a fire in his eyes when finally he set her lips free and said:

"I have to leave you, my darling. There are so many things I have to do before tomorrow, before we can go away in peace on our honeymoon."

His arms tightened as he said:

"Nothing and nobody is going to stop us from

being alone together, when I can make you realise that you are mine and I love you more than life itself."

"I can never... forget that you ... offered your life for . . . mine," Xenia whispered.

"Forget that," the King said. "Forget everything that happened. You know we must never speak of it. At the same time, in the future, my precious one, there must be no secrets between us."

He did not know of the fundamental secret there was already between them, Xenia thought wildly, and for one moment she wondered if she should tell him the truth.

Then she knew it would not only be disloyal to Johanna but would solve nothing.

He was obliged to marry not just her cousin but the daughter of the Arch-Duke Frederich of Prussen.

However much he might love her, however much he might wish, if he learnt the truth, to keep her as his wife, it would be impossible because two other countries were involved, Prussen and Slovia.

Because she felt it was for the last time, Xenia pressed herself closer to him.

"Kiss me again ... István, please ... kiss me once ... again."

"Not once," he replied, "this is just the first of a thousand kisses I shall give you, my dearest darling, my little love, my perfect, wonderful wife-to-be."

He kissed her passionately; then, as Xenia knew it was as agonising for him to leave her as for her to see him go, they walked back together to the Palace.

As she went in through the window of the Salon he left her.

It was difficult to hear anything that was said to her after she joined the party and it was the Dowager Duchess who finally suggested she should go to bed.

"You have a long day before you tomorrow, my dear."

She walked with Xenia to the door, and when they were out of hearing of anyone else she said:

"I cannot tell you what it means to me to see
István so happy. You have changed him, Johanna,
and we are all of us very, very grateful."

"Thank . . . you," Xenia replied.

There was a sob in the words as she slipped away
alone and up the Grand Staircase to bed.

Chapter Six

Driving towards the Cathedral, with the crowd cheering wildly on either side of the route, Xenia felt that she was not only in a dream but also that she must do something about it.

Every moment before she left the Palace for the Cathedral she had expected Johanna to arrive.

She had even sent downstairs three times to ask if there was "a lady from England" to see her.

The answer each time had been "no," and there was nothing she could do but allow Margit to dress her in the beautiful diamond-embroidered wedding-gown that had been, by great good fortune, packed in Johanna's luggage.

Xenia realised that she must have bought it in Paris and had doubtless meant to take it to Prussen where, the Ambassador of that country, who was sitting beside her, had told her the marriage had originally been intended to take place.

"I do not know what His Highness the Arch-Duke will say," he kept repeating in his monotonous German voice. "He will blame me for this unseemly haste, *Mein Prinzessin,* and what can I answer?"

"You must tell him the truth, Herr Winhofenberg," Xenia replied when she could concentrate enough to listen to what he was saying.

It seemed to her that the only thing of which

she was fully conscious was that she was to marry the King and would be with him for a little longer than she had imagined last night would be possible.

The crowds were cheering with a spontaneity which she knew was due not only to the King's new-found popularity but also her own.

There were quite a number of banners being carried by the crowd with SHE CARES! and GOD SAVE OUR QUEEN WHO CARES FOR US! printed on them.

The thousands of children lining the route threw bunches of flowers towards her carriage, which she was sure was on the instigation of their parents.

The newspapers had for the last two days been so filled with excitement over the building of a women's and children's Hospital that it had almost superseded the astonishment over the King's reductions in taxes and his promise of help for industry.

'Whatever else I have done in this very short time, I have at least brought him and his people together,' Xenia thought.

The word "together" made her feel as if a voice asked: "And what about you?" But she knew the answer to that.

Even if she was married to him, she thought, she would have no security of tenure and Johanna when she arrived would automatically take what was her rightful place.

"This enthusiasm is very gratifying, *Mein Prinzessin*," the Prussen Ambassador murmured as the crowds grew thicker as they reached the streets of the city.

It was then that Xenia saw on the wall of a windowless building an enormous poster.

It was a picture of a woman wearing a short, red peasant-skirt and kicking her leg and throwing back her sensuous body in an attitude of abandonment.

At the top of the poster Xenia read: COME AND SEE ELGA IN THE FOLLIES OF MOLNÁR.

Xenia stared at it and for a moment the smile

with which she had acknowledged the cheers faded from her face.

So that was Elga!

She had almost forgotten about her and the King's involvement with her in these last two days of dramatic events.

The poster made it clear that she was not only very attractive but also very vivacious.

'So that is the sort of woman the King really likes!' Xenia thought.

She felt she would have nothing in common with a woman who she now knew was a Music-Hall dancer.

"Elga! Elga!"

The name repeated itself as the State Coach carried her on, and even the cheers of the crowd seemed to repeat the name in her ears.

Yet, by the time they reached the Cathedral, Xenia had other things to think about.

Johanna, she was sure, had seen many Royal Weddings and perhaps as a bride's-maid had taken part in some, but Xenia had not only never seen one but could not remember her mother telling her what happened.

She looked towards the Prussen Ambassador as if for guidance.

Then she felt anything he could tell her would not only be long-winded and tedious, but she would find it hard to follow what he was saying in his guttural German.

The State Coach, decorated with dolphins and mermaids in glittering gold, drew up at the door of the Cathedral.

As Xenia stepped out, the noise of the crowd seemed to deaden even the thoughts in her mind and she suddenly felt helpless and frightened.

The train of her wedding-gown, which attached at her waist, was very long and bordered with ermine, and it was to be carried by four pages dressed in seventeenth-century costume.

Because there had been no time to arrange it she was to have no bride's-maids, but Madame Gyula would act as Matron-of-Honour and take her bouquet when she reached the Chancel steps.

Desperately, feeling almost as if she were drowning in an unknown sea that was buffeting her with waves of indecision and fear, Xenia remembered that during the Service the King would crown her Queen.

She wondered what would happen if at the very moment that she became Queen of Luthenia she was denounced as an imposter.

She had a feeling that the crowd who were cheering her so vivaciously might instead be ready to tear her to pieces.

What was more important, all the good she had done in helping the King would be lost forever.

'No-one will ever know,' she thought confidently, and realised that the Prussen Ambassador was offering her his arm to escort her up the aisle.

The organ, which had been playing softly, changed to a triumphant march and they started to move through the packed congregation whose colourful gowns and sparkling jewels swung in a dazzling kaleidoscope before Xenia's eyes.

The walk to the Chancel seemed interminable. In front of her were the Bishops and the Clergy in their gold-encrusted vestments, preceded by a jewelled cross which seemed to catch the sunlight which was streaming in through the stained-glass windows.

'This cannot be taking place! What will happen when Johanna arrives?' Xenia silently asked herself.

She had a sudden impulse to drop the Ambassador's arm and run away to hide herself.

How could she carry on with a pretence which had turned into something so serious that she felt she was making a mockery of everything which was sacred not only in the Sacrament of marriage but also of the crowning of a Queen?

Then as they reached the Chancel steps she saw the King.

He turned to look at her and as she perceived the expression on his face everything was swept from her mind but him.

Her fears vanished and as she reached his side she felt as if they met each other across eternity, and all this had happened before.

They were together, they had found each other, and nothing else was of any consequence.

In that moment she felt a sense of security and happiness as if he held her in his arms.

She could feel him close beside her, and she felt too as if there was the pressure of his lips on hers.

When the King took her hand and put the wedding-ring on her finger she felt a thrill run through her and thought that he must be aware of it.

"I love you!" she wanted to say. "I love you more than life itself!"

She knew that if he asked it of her she would die for him.

After that she seemed to be enveloped in a golden cloud as she repeated all the responses that were required.

Then she knelt and the diamond tiara she was wearing was removed, and as the King placed the Queen's Crown on her head she wanted to tell him that she was at his feet as his slave for all time.

The Service was very long but to Xenia it passed quickly because she was beside the King and could think of nothing else.

Then at last, after the blessing, the King gave her his arm and they proceeded down the aisle of the Cathedral while the gentlemen bowed their heads and the ladies swept to the ground with a lovely, graceful gesture, looking like a field of corn waving in the wind.

Waiting for them outside in the sunshine was not the closed State Coach in which Xenia had travelled to the Cathedral but an open carriage decorated with flowers and drawn by six snow-white horses.

Xenia was helped in and her long train was arranged on the seat opposite. Then the King sat down beside her.

She thought that in his white tunic and plumed hat he looked more handsome, more authoritative, more commanding, and more irresistibly attractive than he had ever done before.

It would have been impossible to speak above the noise of the crowd, but as the coach moved off the King took Xenia's hand in his and raised it to his lips.

She felt herself tremble at the gesture, and then because she knew it was expected of them she waved with her other hand at the crowd while still holding tightly on to the King.

Now the flowers which the children had brought not only strewed the roadway but many of them were thrown into the carriage.

Soon Xenia and the King were knee-deep in fragrant blossoms. Some of the petals were caught in Xenia's veil and in the King's golden epaulettes.

As they drove along there were no dark, sinister-looking men with folded arms, no dissenting banners, no boos or hostile shouts.

It was applause all the way, and the wildly enthusiastic crowd round the Palace was only with difficulty held back by the troops.

As the carriage drew up at the steps the King asked:

"Are you tired, my darling? It was a long ordeal but you came through it magnificently!"

Xenia turned to look at him. Her heart was in her eyes, but there were no words with which she could express what she felt.

As if he understood, the King said:

"We still have the wedding-banquet ahead of us before we can be alone. Tomorrow I am taking you away on our honeymoon."

Xenia drew in her breath.

She wondered what tomorrow would bring. But there was no time to think of anything, for their guests were waiting for them, and the first person to kiss Xenia with tears in her eyes was the Dowager Duchess.

She, with the King's other relatives and most of the guests at the State Banquet had returned to the Palace by a quicker route.

The long Hall of Mirrors had been converted into a Banqueting-Hall because it was the largest room in the Palace.

A table ran the whole length of it and the gold ornaments and white flowers which decorated it were reflected and rereflected on the mirrored walls.

Xenia had only a few moments in which the Mistress of the Robes removed the heavy crown from her head and replaced it with the diamond tiara which she had worn on her way to the Cathedral.

It was lighter and, she thought secretly, far more becoming.

With her veil falling on either side of her face, she looked ethereal and very like the Fairy Princess she had imagined herself to be.

She looked at her reflection in the mirror and thought that unlike Cinderella the hour of midnight had not struck and she was married—yes, actually married to Prince Charming!

"I love him! I love him!" Xenia whispered to herself. "Please, God, let me stay with him a little while longer."

Today for the first time at a formal meal in the Palace she was seated beside him at the head of the table.

As speech followed speech, she thought that those who made them were speaking to him not only with a new sincerity but also with a note of respect in their voices that had not been there before.

'Mr. Donington was right,' Xenia thought. 'He will make a brilliant King and he will keep the balance of power without any difficulty.'

The King's speech was brief. After thanking everyone there for supporting him, he said:

"There is no need for me to tell you that much that has happened in the last few days is due to the inspiration and strength I have received from my wife.

"If in the future I can serve you as I wish to do, if together we can make Luthenia a country of great importance not only to us but also in the world, it will be because the Queen believes that miracles are possible, and this, in the history of our country, is a miracle."

He said little more before he sat down, but Xenia could still hear the note in his voice when he had called her his "wife."

She had hoped that after the dinner was over their guests would leave, but there was still the Reception.

This was for those who were not important enough to be invited to the State Banquet but were of enough consequence that they must be entertained at the Palace on such an important day.

The two great Salons which connected with each other were overflowing with the numbers of people waiting for them there, and there was also a buffet provided outside in the garden.

It was not yet dark, but the fairy-lights bordered the paths and flower-beds and lanterns hung from the branches of the trees.

The fountain was lit so that the water flying high into the air held every colour of the rainbow.

It was all very lovely, but again Xenia could think of nothing but the man moving beside her as they circulated amongst their guests.

Her long train had been removed and her gossamer fine gown now had a short train at the back.

She knew without conceit that she not only looked very lovely and ethereal but that the diamanté which covered her dress made her shine even amongst the other lights in the garden.

There were so many people to talk to, so many compliments to accept, that it was almost in surprise that Xenia heard the Count come to the King's side and say:

"It is ten-thirty, Your Majesty."

"Then we can say good-night," the King said with a note of eagerness in his voice that Xenia did not miss.

He offered her his arm and the gentlemen-in-waiting in the Court went ahead of them.

Now in a small procession, the Count bringing up the rear, they walked back towards the Palace, with their guests curtseying and bowing on either side of them.

Back in the Salon, they said not only good-night but good-bye to the relatives and the Royal guests.

They were to leave the following day, but officially even though they were in the Palace the King and Queen were then on their honeymoon.

"Good-bye, my dearest Johanna," the Dowager Grand Duchess said. "God bless you and István as I know He has already done."

Xenia and the King moved from the Salon into the Hall.

She thought this would mean that she was to be alone with the King immediately, but she found that the Mistress of the Robes and five other Ladies of the Bed-Chamber must by tradition escort her to her bed-room.

The King kissed her hand and she walked up the staircase alone, not wishing to be separated from him but knowing she must do what was expected of her.

When they reached the Bed-Chamber, the Mistress of the Robes curtseyed and made a speech asking the blessing of God on her marriage, combined with the hope that there would be heirs to the throne to follow in His Majesty's footsteps.

It was a little embarrassing and when the speech was over each Lady in turn not only curtseyed but kissed her hand and vowed herself to the Queen's service.

133

Barbara Cartland

Then at last they were gone and Xenia let Margit
undress her.

It was then that almost for the first time she decided she must tell the King the truth.

It was one thing to act the part of Johanna, to
accept the wedding-ring and the crown on her be-
half, but quite another to allow the King to make
love to her believing she was another woman.

Xenia was very innocent, and she had no idea exactly what happened when a man and a woman
became one, as she was told they did in the Marriage-
Service.

But she knew that it might produce a child and
she asked herself in a sudden panic what would happen if when Johanna arrived and she returned to
England she found that she was to have a baby.

The thought had never struck her before simply
because she had never anticipated for a moment that
she would get as far as marrying the King.

She had been so sure that Johanna would be
aware of what was happening in Luthenia and would
arrive long before there was any possibility of her becoming the wife of the man she now loved.

"I must tell him the truth before he touches me,"
she told herself, and trembled because she thought
he might be angry.

In fact she was quite sure he would be very angry.
What man would not be, having been deceived and
to all intents and purposes made to feel a fool?

"But I have helped him, I have made him popu-
lar. Perhaps if I had not been here he would not have
had the courage to fight the Prime Minister.'

Xenia's excuses seemed very plausible when she
rehearsed them in her mind, but at the same time
there was still the personal element, which was something very different.

The King had kissed her and it had been the
most wonderful, perfect, glorious thing that could
ever have happened to her.

Perhaps he had felt the same way when he

134

kissed Elga, she told herself, and for him, whatever he might have said, there had been nothing unique or sensational about it, as it had seemed to her.

But a kiss was one thing; to make love was quite another.

"I must tell him! I must!" Xenia admonished herself.

She found with hardly being aware of it that she was wearing a nightgown and Margit was waiting for her to get into bed.

The huge draped bed, with its ornate canopy, soft, lace-edged pillows, and embroidered coverlet, had a significance that made Xenia as she climbed into it feel pulsatingly shy.

Margit pulled the sheets into place, laid Xenia's negligé over a chair, and turned out the lights.

All that was left was a candelabrum with three candles at the bed-side and they were veiled from Xenia by the folds of the curtains.

'Perhaps it will be easier to tell him if I am in the shadows,' she thought.

She pressed back against the pillows, trying to fortify herself against what lay ahead, vividly aware that her heart was fluttering in her breast and her fingers were cold.

She heard the communicating door which joined the King's and Queen's Suites together open for the first time since she had been in the Palace, and she found it hard to breathe as the King came into the room.

He was wearing a long blue robe which nearly touched the ground and made him seem even taller and more impressive than when he was wearing his ordinary clothes.

As he drew nearer to the bed Xenia saw that the lines of cynicism had gone from his face.

Instead, his eyes had a strange excitement in them so that it was hard to recognise the man who had met her only a week ago, looking so bored and indifferent.

Barbara Cartland

He came to the bed-side and looked at her sitting upright, her red hair falling over her shoulders and down to her waist, the thin, lace-inserted lawn of her nightgown doing little to conceal the soft curves of her breasts.

He stood looking at her as, unable to speak, she twisted her fingers together.

"Do you know how beautiful you are?" he said. "I have longed to see your hair like that."

Xenia knew that this was the moment when she must tell him the truth, but somehow her breath seemed to be constricted in her throat.

It would be easier, she thought frantically, if the King did not look at her so that she could see the love in his eyes and what she thought too was a touch of fire.

"István . . ." she began at last.

The sound was so faint that she felt he could not have heard it.

But he had, for he sat down on the side of the bed facing her, and she knew it was because he wanted to go on looking at her, at her red hair shining in the candlelight, and at her lips, which were trembling because she was afraid.

"I love you!" he said before she could speak. "God, how much I love you! I never believed it possible to feel like this about any woman, least of all you!"

He put out his arms to draw her to him and as he did so he said:

"I am in love—wildly, crazily in love, my beautiful wife!"

At the touch of his hands Xenia found her voice.

"I . . . I have . . . something to . . . t-tell you."

She felt him stiffen, and because of her love for him she knew with a perception that was irrefutable that he was afraid of what he was about to hear.

Because she loved him so overwhelmingly she was aware that he was expecting her to say something about the lover to whom he had referred when greeting her on the train.

136

"What do you want to say?" he asked.

Now his tone was different and his hands rested on the sheet in front of him, no longer touching her bare arms.

Xenia drew in her breath.

How could she tell him? she asked herself. How could she sweep the happiness from his eyes?

How could she spoil this moment of ecstasy?

She loved him so overwhelmingly, so completely and absolutely with her mind, her body, and her soul, that she knew she would kill herself to save him one moment's pain or distress.

This was his wedding-night, and because he had trusted her, because he had let her guide and inspire him, the whole situation in Luthenia had been changed.

Quite suddenly she knew she could not do it, not tonight at any rate ... and perhaps tomorrow would never come.

Perhaps they would go to sleep and never wake up.... Perhaps anything might happen ... or nothing....

What she could not do was to sweep away the happiness on the face of the man she loved or to tell him that he had been deceived.

"I am waiting," the King said.

She thought the cynical lines were already back on his face and there was no longer a glitter in his eyes.

She made a little movement towards him, not consciously willing it, but because she wanted the closeness of him so desperately.

"I ... I wanted to t-tell you," she whispered, "that I love you ... but ... I do not know ... what to ... do."

The words seemed to come from her lips without her choosing them or knowing what she was saying.

"What do you mean—you do not know what to do?" the King asked.

"I—it is just that ... I ..."

She could not find the words to express what she was trying to say, and because she was shy she could no longer meet his eyes and tried to hide her face against his shoulder.

His arms went round her, then he said:

"I must be very stupid, but I do not understand what you are trying to tell me."

She could not answer and after a second he put his fingers under her chin and turned her face up to his.

"Look at me, Xenia," he said. "What do you mean —you do not know what to do?"

"I . . . love you . . . all I know is . . . that I love you!"

He looked at her for a long moment, then he said:

"I suppose I should have suspected—and you must have thought me very dense—but I believed those lies you told me about an English lover. And yet when I kissed you I would have sworn before God Himself that nobody had ever kissed you before."

"Nobody . . . ever . . . has!" Xenia whispered.

Something seemed to break in the King, and in a voice that had a wild note of triumph in it he said:

"I was right! Oh, my darling, I was right! You are mine as I have wanted you to be!"

Then as if he would sweep away the last doubts he said:

"Tell me—tell me by all that you hold sacred—as if you were in the presence of God Himself, that you have never belonged to another man, that no man has ever touched you."

"Th-that is . . . true," Xenia whispered again.

Almost before the words left her lips, the King was kissing her, his mouth holding her captive as he pushed her back against the pillows.

She felt the wild exhilaration he was feeling sweep over her so that she ceased to think but could only feel the wonder of his lips and the thrill that ran pulsating through her body at the touch of his hands.

She felt as if flames were being lit inside her, the flames she had seen in the King's eyes, which she knew were echoed in her own.

"I love you! I love you!"

The words seemed to whirl round them, and then the King was close beside her and she could feel his heart beating against hers.

She knew then that this was what she had longed for, this was what she knew was love in all its perfection; the love she had thought never to find, but which was not only his arms but was all of him.

She felt his lips on her eyes, her cheeks, her neck, and then he was kissing her breasts.

The whole world seemed to be filled with fire and the songs of angels; and they too, as one person, were part of the Divine. . . .

* * *

Somewhere very far away Xenia heard the sound of marching feet and knew it was the sentries guarding the Palace.

She turned her head against the King's shoulder and felt him kiss her forehead.

There was still a golden light percolating through the curtain beside them, but it was much fainter than it had been before and Xenia thought the candles must be guttering low.

"I love . . . you!" she murmured.

They were the same words she had said a thousand times, yet she wanted to go on saying them.

"I worship you!" the King replied. "And I had no idea it was possible to be so happy and still be on this earth."

"You really are . . . happy?" Xenia asked. "I did not do anything . . . wrong?"

The King gave a little laugh.

"Wrong, my precious one? No-one could be more perfect, more right in every way."

She gave a little sigh of sheer happiness as he went on:

"We are right for each other. You are mine and I am yours and nothing else in the world is of any consequence."

"That is . . . what I feel," Xenia said with a sigh.

"Oh, my wonderful darling, I have so much to teach you about love, and so much love to prove, that I very much doubt if it can all be done in one lifetime."

Far away, on the very edge of her consciousness, Xenia remembered that they would not be together for a lifetime or perhaps very much longer. Then she forced the thought from her.

This was her hour, this was her night and his, and nothing should spoil it.

As she pressed herself impulsively a little closer to him he said:

"That is how I want you to be, against my heart and in my heart, and mine until the world comes to an end. Then, I believe, my adorable one, we will be together in a Paradise of our own."

"I am in Paradise . . . now," Xenia answered. "When you were loving me I wished I could . . . die because I did not believe it . . . possible to feel any . . . happier "

"You will not die but live," the King said. "This is only the beginning. You are like a flower, my darling one, which is still in bud."

He kissed her forehead again and said:

"I cannot believe anyone could be more lovely than you are at this moment, and yet I have a feeling that our love will give you a new beauty because now, my wonderful little wife, you are a woman!"

Xenia blushed and hid her face against him, and he said:

"My woman! Mine! Oh, my precious, if you only knew what it means to know that all those lies you told me were untrue!"

He made a sound that was almost a laugh and said:

140

"I am well aware why you told me them. You had heard about Elga and you felt you must hold your own and also perhaps make me aware of what a fool I was."

"Did you . . . love her?" Xenia asked, remembering the abandoned posture on the poster.

"No, of course not!" the King replied. "She was just a 'passing fancy' that was blown up out of all proportion by those who hated me, and, I am quite sure, it was at the instigation of the Prime Minister."

His arms tightened round Xenia as he said:

"Because you had heard of the woman, it ruined our relationship from the moment we met, even allowing for the fact that we were both being pressurised into a marriage we neither of us wanted."

"Could we . . . forget it . . . just for . . . tonight?" Xenia asked.

"We will forget it forever!" the King answered. "You belong to me, my darling. I can still hardly believe, though my lips tell me that it is true, that you had never been kissed before that magical, wonderful moment under the Falls."

"I did not know a . . . kiss could be so . . . ecstatic! Or . . ."

She paused.

"Or?" the King prompted, and she whispered:

"Making love could be so . . . perfect . . . so glorious . . . and a part of . . . God."

"That is how it is because we love each other," the King said. "I promise you one thing, my darling, there will never be anyone else in either of our lives."

His lips sought hers as he added:

"For one thing, I shall be very jealous! You are far too beautiful for any man's peace of mind."

Xenia wanted to say that as far as she was concerned she would never want any other man in her life, but the King's lips were becoming more insistent, more passionate, and his hands were touching her again.

The little ripples of fire were running through her

veins and her breath was coming quickly through her lips.

All she could say, not in words but with her mind, her body, and her soul, was:

"I love . . . you! I love . . . you!"

❋   ❋   ❋

Xenia awoke to find the sun shining between the curtains.

'I am married!' she thought.

She turned towards the King but the place where he had slept was empty, and she felt a sense of disappointment which was almost one of dismay.

Then she heard him come back into the room through the communicating door.

He was dressed, and he went to a window and pulled back the curtains. As the sunshine flowed in, golden and compelling, he turned to look at her with a smile on his lips.

"Are you awake, my precious?"

"I had just . . . woken up to . . . find you gone, and thought I had . . . lost you."

There was a throb in her voice that pleased him and he walked to the bed, thinking as he did so that he had never seen a woman look so lovely in the morning.

Xenia's skin was dazzlingly white, her red hair was streaming over the pillow, and her eyes, still a little hazy with sleep, were vividly green.

He stood looking down at her for a moment before he asked:

"Are you real? I feel you are like a nymph from the sea or from the woods who will suddenly vanish back to where you have come from and I shall be alone again."

Xenia felt with a pang of her heart that this was something which indeed would happen, and perhaps because they were so closely attuned to each other she had put the idea into his head.

142

"What are we...going to do...today?" she asked.

"I would like to answer that by saying that I am coming back to bed to make love to you. I assure you there is nothing I want more."

He sat down facing her as he spoke and put out his hand to touch her hair.

"What are we...really going to...do?"

There was a sense of urgency in her voice because she had to know.

"I have arranged, much against my wishes, a Privy Council meeting for this morning," the King replied. "Then, whatever anyone may say, whatever urgent matters are outstanding, we are leaving on our honeymoon."

"Where are we going?" Xenia enquired.

"It is a secret. I have a surprise for you. It would spoil it if you knew."

She gave a little cry of excitement.

"I love surprises...if they are...nice."

"This will be very *nice*," the King said, accentuating the word, "but I can think of a more descriptive adjective for being alone with you without any pomp and ceremony and certainly without a lady-in-waiting."

"All I...want is to be with...you," Xenia whispered.

There was a little note of passion in her voice that was unmistakable and the King bent nearer as he said:

"If you look at me like that and say such things there will be no Privy Council meeting. Or they can wait where they are until tomorrow."

The fire was back in his eyes and because she could not help herself she put her arms round his neck.

"Do you still love me?" she questioned.

"Do you want me to prove it?" the King answered. "It is something I am very willing to do."

143

His lips came down on hers and for a moment she could not answer.

Then with an almost superhuman effort she put her hands on his chest to push him away from her.

"You must do what is . . . right."

"What is right is for me to kiss you!"

His lips were demanding. She knew that she had excited him and that he wanted her as indeed she wanted him.

Then she turned her face to one side, away from his lips.

"Hurry," she said. "Hurry with the Privy Council and let us get away . . . quickly on our honeymoon, and please . . . please, István, darling . . . do not let anything disturb us, however . . . urgent it may appear."

"I will make sure of that," the King answered.

As she turned her face round to his, he said in a voice she hardly recognised:

"It is agony to leave you, you know that, and my whole body burns for you. I think too, my precious, that there is a little fire burning in you that has not been there before."

Xenia looked into his eyes and he saw the answer without her speaking.

He kissed her once again, then walked from the room as if he was a soldier going on parade.

Xenia gave a sigh of sheer joy.

Never had she believed it was possible to feel as happy as she did at this moment, knowing that the King had awakened a thousand different sensations within her that she had never felt before.

This was love as it was meant to be; love which not only united a man and a woman as human beings, but which had taken them up to Heaven so that their very passion for each other was sanctified and made holy.

'He is so wonderful!' she thought.

Margit brought in her breakfast, and she had her bath thinking only of the King and wondering where he had planned they should go where no-one would find them.

'The people are beginning to trust him,' she thought, 'and without the Prime Minister to stir up trouble, everything will carry on peacefully until he returns.'

When she had finished drying herself Margit brought her a wrap of pale blue satin trimmed with frill upon frill of real lace.

Xenia put it on to sit at the dressing-table while Margit arranged her hair, choosing a style that was young because she knew that was how the King would want her to look.

And yet he had said she had become a woman!

She stared at her reflection in the mirror to observe any difference, thinking there should be an enormous one.

But the eyes that looked back at her not only were very green but alight with a happiness that had never been there before.

She thought too that her lips were fuller and very curved because all through the night the King had kissed them.

Margit had just finished putting the last pin in her hair when there was a knock at the door.

She crossed the room to open it. There was a whispered conversation, then she returned to Xenia and said:

"There is a lady from England to see Your Majesty. The Major Domo thought that as you asked for her so often yesterday Your Majesty would be expecting her, and she is waiting outside."

"Not outside, but in!" a voice said from the door.

Without turning her head, Xenia knew who had spoken.

It was Johanna—a day and a night late!

Chapter Seven

Margit moved towards the door.

"If Your Majesty will ring when you want me ..."
she murmured, curtseying, and left the room.

Xenia turned round.

Johanna was standing at the far end of the bed-
room just inside the door and Xenia saw that she was
dressed as a widow.

Her gown, far too elegant for anyone who was
deeply bereaved, revealed her slender and graceful
figure and was ornamented with crêpe.

She wore a small crêpe bonnet on her head and
had a crêpe veil which completely covered her face.

She raised this with black-gloved hands and Xenia
saw that she was smiling.

"Here I am!" Johanna exclaimed. "And do not say
that you are surprised to see me."

"Not ... surprised," Xenia managed to reply, "but
I expected you ... yesterday or the ... day before."

Johanna walked towards her and once again it
was as strange as if she were seeing her own reflection
in a mirror.

The mourning might be a clever disguise, but it
accentuated Johanna's white skin, red hair, and green
eyes.

"I thought," Xenia went on, "that you would
read in the newspapers that the King's ... marriage

was to take ... place and would know it was ... imperative that you should come here at ... once."

"I did not see the newspapers for some days," Johanna answered. "I had other things to think about."

She smiled as she spoke, and added:

"Oh, Xenia, I can never thank you enough for taking my place. I have been so happy and had such a heavenly time with Robert."

There was almost a dreamy note in her voice. Then in a very different tone she said:

"But you must hurry! He is waiting for you downstairs and your train leaves in an hour."

"M-my ... train?" Xenia echoed almost stupidly.

"Robert has your ticket and he will see you off. He also has the money I promised you."

"B-but ... I ..." Xenia began, then her voice died away.

There was nothing she could say, nothing she could do. This was the moment when the fairy-story came to an end.

Feeling as if it was difficult to move, she rose to her feet.

"As you are not dressed, you have nothing to do but put on my clothes," Johanna was saying. "You will have to undo my gown at the back."

She pulled off her widow's bonnet as she spoke and turned round so that Xenia could undo the little silk-covered buttons which fastened her gown.

"You ... have been ... happy?" she asked.

"Marvellously, blissfully happy!" Johanna replied. "I love Robert and to me he is the most attractive man in the world!"

"Then why ... why do you not ... stay with him?"

Xenia could not help asking the question which seemed almost to burst from her lips.

Johanna put up both her hands in a gesture of self-protection.

147

"Do not say it," she begged. "I have listened to nothing else from Robert all the time we were coming here."

She gave a little laugh that was almost a sob.

"You do not understand, nor does Robert, but I cannot—I will not vanish into obscurity like your mother did."

She spoke violently. Then after a moment she added:

"If I had known I could feel like this when I first knew Robert, I would have run away with him. But I would have made it quite clear that I would remain a Princess and would not have allowed my relatives to hush everything up and treat me as if I were something untouchable."

"Is it . . . too late . . . now?" Xenia asked in a low voice.

"Much too late!" Johanna replied. "And how could we ever explain your presence here?"

The words brought Xenia a forcible reminder of all she had done for Luthenia.

"Listen, Johanna," she said quickly, "for I have so much to tell . . ."

"But there is no time for me to listen to it," Johanna interrupted. "Robert is waiting, and I understand the King has a Privy Council meeting, but they do not necessarily last for long."

"We were . . . leaving on our . . . h-honeymoon."

"Well, that is something I have no intention of doing," Johanna replied. "As long as I remain in Molnár, there is some chance of my seeing Robert."

"He is . . . staying in the . . . city?" Xenia enquired.

"For the time being," Johanna said. "But how can I let him go?"

The question was almost a cry. At the same time, she had stepped out of her gown and thrown it on the chair, and now she was taking off the beautiful lace-trimmed underclothes of which there were so many duplicates in her luggage.

She pulled off her chemise; then, naked, she turned to look at herself in the mirror.

"Robert thinks I am as beautiful as a Greek goddess," she said, "and I suppose he would think the same of you. I am glad he is not accompanying you back to England."

Xenia told herself she had no interest in what Lord Gratton thought. Aloud she said:

"You must help István, Johanna. He needs help."

"István can look after himself!" Johanna retorted. "And I gather from the newspapers which I read as we crossed the border that you have been very busy with Hospitals and such things. I cannot tell you how much they bore me!"

"But . . . Johanna . . . they are necessary . . . desperately necessary for Luthenia."

Johanna did not answer and Xenia thought despairingly that she was not interested.

Almost automatically she put on the clothes which Johanna had discarded and her cousin slipped her nightgown over her head and over it the blue silk wrap trimmed with lace.

"Robert has some luggage for you," she said. "I had to buy a lot of things in one way or another, and I expect you will find them useful."

"I . . . I have nothing . . . else."

"Then you will appreciate them," Johanna smiled, "and they are quite as attractive, although not to be compared with all the things I bought in Paris."

She glanced towards the wardrobe as she spoke, where Margit had left the doors open, waiting for Xenia to choose what she would wear.

Then, without being asked, Johanna buttoned Xenia's gown up at the back and picked up the crêpe bonnet she had thrown to the floor.

"It was a clever disguise, was it not?" she asked. "Actually it was Robert who thought of it. He said it would be impossible for me to arrive in Luthenia with everyone thinking I was you."

149

Barbara Cartland

"I think I ... ought to tell you ..." Xenia began.

Even as she spoke she knew it was somehow impossible to say to Johanna that she was deeply in love with the King and he with her.

She knew too that she ought to tell her that they had been together last night and she was in fact his wife not only legally but because they loved each other.

Yet the words would not come to her lips, and as she hesitated, trying to express that which seemed inexpressible, Johanna looked at the clock and gave a little scream.

"You will miss your train," she cried, "and you know as well as I do that the sooner you are out of the country the better!"

She picked up her black gloves and with them a handbag which she had carried on her wrist when she came into the room.

"Give me your wedding-ring," she said, "and hurry downstairs. Robert is waiting for you in the carriage and he will explain everything."

As she spoke she put Xenia's bonnet on her head, tied the ribbons under her chin, and kissed her cheek before she pulled the veil over her face.

Xenia took off her wedding-ring and as Johanna took it she said:

"Thank you, kindest, most accommodating of cousins. It is sad that we shall never see each other again, but I shall always be grateful for what you have done for me."

She put out her hand as she spoke and rang a little gold bell which stood on the dressing-table. Almost as soon as it tinkled, the door opened and Margit returned.

"Show my friend, Mrs. Cresswell, to the top of the stairs," Johanna said.

"Very good, Your Majesty."

Xenia had half-expected Margit to notice the difference in her mistress, to think perhaps that her voice had changed since she had left the room.

150

But it was obvious that Margit accepted Johanna without question, and with a feeling of helplessness Xenia could only follow her to the door.

There she turned and curtseyed to Johanna, who gave her a little wave of her hand.

Then Margit led her to the top of the staircase to where the Major Domo was waiting to escort her down the staircase and out onto the steps.

Xenia could see a closed carriage waiting and outside the gold-tipped gates there was a crowd ready to wave to their King and Queen as they left for their honeymoon.

It was like having a thousand daggers turned in her heart to know that he would drive away with Johanna while she was scuttling out of the country, hidden beneath a black veil.

Slowly, step by step, she walked towards the closed carriage; then a footman opened the door and she climbed into it.

There was a man inside it but he did not speak until as the horses moved off he said:

"Johanna has doubtless thanked you for what you have done for us and I would like to thank you too."

Xenia turned her face to look at him through the darkness of her veil and saw that he was obviously English and good-looking. At the same time, she wondered how Johanna could prefer him to the King.

"You have no need to . . . thank me," she said after a moment. "It has been an . . . experience I shall n-never forget."

Despite her resolution to speak calmly, there was an unmistakable sob behind her words. As if Lord Gratton understood what she was feeling, he said in an impersonal tone:

"I have with me your ticket to England. I have already arranged for your sleeping compartment on the train, and a private cabin in the cross-Channel Steamer."

"Thank . . . you," Xenia murmured.

"Johanna told me that she was giving you two hundred pounds for the part you have played in this masquerade," Lord Gratton went on, "but because I personally owe you so much I have added another two hundred pounds, and it is here in this envelope."

He passed it to Xenia as he spoke, which left him still with another paper in his hand.

She put the money in the satin bag which hung from her wrist and when she had done so Lord Gratton said:

"You will need a passport to get back into England and it will also be inspected when the train enters Austria. I have had it made out in the name of 'Mrs. Cresswell.' As you are dressed as a widow, it ought to show your married status."

"I . . . understand," Xenia said.

"There will be no difficulties, of course," Lord Gratton continued, "but if by any chance there are, you will not be able to communicate with Johanna. I shall be staying at the Crown Hotel in Molnár for the next week or so."

"Is that . . . wise?" Xenia asked.

"Wise or not, it is what I am going to do," Lord Gratton replied. "I must be near Johanna—I cannot bear to leave her."

He spoke with a sudden note of passion in his voice that aroused Xenia's sympathy.

She could understand so well what he was feeling.

How could she bear to leave the King? How could she go away like this? And he would never understand why she had changed.

She knew that Johanna, loving Lord Gratton as she did, would never give the King the love he had received from "Xenia."

He would be puzzled, bewildered, and because she thought he would be hurt it was an agony that was inexpressible to know that the carriage was carrying her nearer and nearer to the station.

She was to start on the long journey which would

take her out of István's country and out of his life and
they would never see each other again.

It was perhaps because of her silence, or perhaps
it was because Lord Gratton was suffering so in-
tensely himself, that he guessed what had occurred
since she had come to Luthenia.

"You love the King?" he questioned in a low voice.

Xenia nodded her head, for she could not trust
herself to speak.

"Then we are both in the same boat," he remarked
bitterly.

"There was no time to talk to Johanna," Xenia
said, "but will you beg her to be ... kind to the ...
King? To ... help him? He needs help with ... all
he has to do."

"I gather from the newspapers that he has already
made some very drastic changes in the country,
which will certainly receive the approval of Great
Britain."

"That is what I ... hope," Xenia replied, "but
there is still a ... great deal to be done."

Lord Gratton was silent for a moment, then he
said:

"I can see you are interested in the things which
never have concerned Johanna. It is a pity we cannot
leave things as they are."

Xenia wanted to agree with him, but she felt
that if she did she would break down and cry.

Instead, with an effort she stared out the window
through her veil and thought it was somehow fitting
that her last sight of Molnár should be veiled in
darkness.

The streets were busy, and although she knew it
was probably just imagination, she thought that the
people looked happier and had a lilt in their walk
which had not been there when she arrived.

Then she told herself it was no use believing
that her going would really make any difference except to the private life of the King.

Her whole being cried out at the thought of being separated from him. Then as she felt as if it was too painful to be borne, the carriage drew up outside the station.

"Your train goes in five minutes' time," Lord Gratton said. "I am afraid it is a very slow one, stopping at every station until it reaches the border, but in Austria you will catch an express which will carry you to Vienna."

'There is no hurry,' Xenia thought.

She had nothing and no-one waiting for her in England, and if she had the choice, the journey could take a month or a year before she reached her native soil and severed her last link with Luthenia.

There was, however nothing she could say as she stepped out of the carriage, and Lord Gratton ordered several trunks that had been strapped on the back of it to be taken by a porter to the Guard's Van of the train.

He and Xenia walked onto the platform, where she found that he had reserved a whole carriage for her.

He handed her into it, tipped the porters generously, and then lifting his hat from his head, he took her hand in his.

"Thank you once again," he said. "If you need me once I am back in London, you can find me at Gratton House, but I do not intend to return until I have to."

That, as Xenia knew, would be when Johanna commanded him to go.

"Thank you for looking after me," she said, "and for the ... money ... it was very ... kind."

"I can never repay you in cash for giving me the happiest time in my life," Lord Gratton said.

There was a note of despair in his voice.

Xenia knew that for him, as for her, everything that made life worth living was over and there was nothing to look forward to in the future but loneliness and despair.

She tried to find words with which to comfort him, but at that moment the Guard blew his whistle, there was the noise of doors being slammed, and Lord Gratton stepped back from beside the carriage.

With a jerk of the wheels and the clang of the coaches the train moved out of the station and Xenia saw Lord Gratton turn and walk away towards the waiting carriage.

It was then that she threw back her veil to take her last look at Molnár.

In a few minutes they were outside the city, where there were the wild flowers growing beside the railway-line, and there was a magnificent view of the valley with the silvery river winding through the centre of it.

The white peaks of the mountains gleamed against the blue sky and made her remember the day she and the King had ridden together.

As Xenia stared for the last time at the picture it all made, the tears came, at first running down her cheeks, then turning to a tempest of weeping which shook her whole body.

It was over!

She had left her heart, her soul, and, she thought, her personality behind her, and all that was left was an empty shell.

"I love you! Oh, István . . . I love you!" she said as she sobbed.

Then she went down into a special hell in which there was no light in the darkness and nothing but despair—a despair which was worse than death.

"At least if István were dead," Xenia told herself, "I should have the hope and faith that one day when I die I will see him again. But as it is, we will each live in different parts of the world, and because he will never know of my very existence, even my thoughts and prayers will not reach him."

She cried until she felt exhausted.

Then she forced herself to wipe her eyes and

look out the window for she knew this would be the last time she would ever see Luthenia.

Ever since they left Molnár the train had been climbing upwards towards the pass in the mountains.

It was, as Lord Gratton had warned Xenia, a very slow train. They stopped at every small way-side station, where sometimes one or two people would get out or a farmer's wife carrying a basket of eggs or chickens would get in.

Then with a bang and a clang they would start off again, only to repeat the process farther along the line.

Later in the day they waited for a long time in a siding to let another train pass.

It was growing hotter and Xenia thought that soon it would be midday and by this time the King and Johanna would have left the Palace.

She had a feeling that whether Johanna wanted to or not, she would be forced into going on their honeymoon as planned, simply because there would be no alternative.

She might want to stay in Molnár in the hope of seeing Lord Gratton, but the King had made all his arrangements and he simply would not understand why there should be any objections from his wife.

His wife!

The words seemed to cut through Xenia's heart.

She was his wife. They had been joined together by the Archbishop and had become one in an act of love that, she knew, also had been sanctified by God.

It had been so perfect, so utterly and completely divine, that even to think of it made her tremble with the sensations the King had aroused in her last night.

"I worship you, my wonderful little wife," he had said to her.

She had felt as if they were sanctified by their love and the fire that he evoked in her was a gift from God.

Now the King would never know, never understand why she had changed, why she no longer sought
his kisses, or why Johanna in her place would turn
away from him.

"Oh, István! István!" she cried out despairingly,
but the only answer was the rumble of the wheels.

* * *

After several hours had passed Xenia realised
she was both hungry and thirsty but she did not dare
to try to buy food at any of the stations at which
they stopped.

It would be too dangerous, she thought, and also
too much of an effort.

There was not really any likelihood that anyone
could look through the thickness of the veil and see
her resemblance to their Queen, but still, it was better to play safe.

She only wished she had asked what time they
would cross the border into Austria.

She knew it would not be long now, because the
train had climbed high up the pass and the land
round them was rocky and mountainous.

As was usual on alpine plateaux, the flowers were
even more brilliant and more profuse than they were
in the valley and Xenia stared at them. If ever she
saw flowers in the future they would remind her of
the King.

She remembered how he had kissed her in the
garden and the fragrance of the roses had been all
round them.

The train stopped at yet another station and Xenia
was sure that this was the Luthenia border. She was
therefore not surprised when a man in uniform
opened the door.

She drew out from her handbag her ticket and
the passport which Lord Gratton had given to her.

The official examined the ticket, then opened
her passport, which was in the shape of a letter.

Surmounted by the Royal Coat-of-Arms, it read:

We, George Leweson Gower Granville Earl Granville a Peer and a Member of Her Britannic's Majesty's Most Honourable Privy Council, Her Majesty's Principal Secretary of State for Foreign Affairs, etc., etc., etc.

Request and require in the Name of Her Majesty all those it may concern to allow Mrs. Xenia Cresswell to pass freely without let or hindrance and to afford her every assistance and protection of which she may stand in need.

Given at Foreign Office, London, on 12th day of June 1883.

Granville.

Beneath the Earl's signature was his personal Coat-of-Arms.

The official read it slowly and asked:

"Will you come with me, please, Madam."

Xenia supposed there must be papers to be signed because she was entering Austria.

Obediently she rose to her feet and the official helped her onto the platform.

There were a number of peasants in their bright red skirts and embroidered blouses standing staring at the train, and several passengers who looked like commercial travellers were boarding it with their luggage.

The official went ahead of Xenia and she followed him inside an attractive building which was painted white and ornamented with window-boxes filled with flowers.

They passed through a corridor in which there were a number of people arguing with a booking-clerk, and the official opened a door at the far end of it.

He stood back for Xenia to enter first and as she did so she realised there was one man in a small room who was standing at a desk.

She looked at him perfunctorily, then felt as if she had been turned to stone.

It was the King who stood there!

The King, dressed not in uniform but in his ordinary clothes, bare-headed, and staring at her in a manner which made her feel as if her heart had stopped beating.

"You are Mrs. Cresswell?"

She could not answer. It was absolutely impossible for her to utter a word and she felt too as if her brain had ceased to function.

She could not even wonder why he was there or why he was asking her questions.

"I understand that you left Molnár in somewhat of a hurry," the King said. "In fact you departed with so much haste that you left something behind."

Xenia stared at him through the darkness of her veil, trying to understand what he was saying, conscious only of her love, which seemed to be welling up inside her like a tidal wave.

She felt the tears prick her eyes and she could only see him through a mist.

"Will you come here?"

As if she were a puppet and he was pulling the strings, she walked towards the desk.

It was only a few steps and yet she felt it was miles away.

She stood in front of him, acutely conscious of his closeness, but she could not speak, could not breathe.

Her mind had been taken from her and it was impossible to think or even to understand what was happening.

"I want you to take off your left glove," the King said.

She wondered why, but because it was so difficult to control her tears she could only obey him dumbly.

She pulled off the black kid glove and when she had done so the King reached out and took her hand in his.

"No wedding-ring?" he asked. "How can you be a married woman without one?"

As he spoke he drew a ring from his waist-coat pocket and put it on her third finger.

It was her own wedding-ring, Xenia knew, but she could not move or take her hand from his.

Then the King released her, and taking the edge of her veil in both of his hands he threw it back from her face.

"Let me look at you, Mrs. Cresswell," he said. "I want to see if you are as beautiful as I remember you to be."

Xenia stared into his eyes and he looked down at her for a long moment.

"Why have you been crying?" he asked.

The tears overflowed as he spoke and ran down her cheeks.

He was waiting for her to answer, and in a voice that seemed to come from very far away she whispered through lips that trembled:

"I thought . . . I would . . . never see you . . . again."

"Did you really think I could lose you?" the King asked, and his arms went round her.

He pulled her against him and as she gave a little gasp his lips came down on hers.

She felt as if she had been swept from the very depths of Hell into Heaven, which was so dazzlingly glorious that she must shut her eyes for fear of being blinded.

The King kissed her until she was one with him again and they were indivisible.

Then at last, in a voice that was curiously unsteady, he asked:

"How could you have done anything so wicked, so utterly and completely abominable, as to try to leave me?"

"I love . . . you! Oh . . . István, I love . . . you!"

Xenia's voice was broken. The tears were still running down her cheeks, but they were tears of happiness.

He kissed her wet eyes, her cheeks, and again her mouth.

"You are mine," he said. "Mine, completely and absolutely, and I can no more lose you than lose my own life."

"B-but . . . Johanna?" Xenia managed to ask.

The King kissed her again before he said:

"You need not worry about Johanna, my precious. She is at this moment on her way to Vienna in the Royal Train with her future husband and is planning the trousseau she will buy in Paris."

Xenia looked at him enquiringly, but he only undid the ribbons beneath her chin, pulled her bonnet with its dark veil from her head, and threw it on the desk.

"I will explain everything," he said, "but first I want to kiss you."

His lips were on hers before he had finished the sentence.

She felt a thrill like shafts of sunlight running through her body, her heart was beating against his, and the wonder of it almost was too glorious to be borne.

Still holding her against him, the King sat down on a chair and pulled her onto his knees.

She hid her face against his neck.

How did . . . you find . . . out?"

The King smiled.

"Did you really think I could be deceived by another woman, even if she was so ridiculously like you?"

"H-how did you . . . know?"

"I admit to being bewildered and astounded for the moment," he replied.

"Tell me . . . please tell me," Xenia begged.

He kissed her cheek, then her lips, before he said:

"When the Privy Council was finished I went to your bed-room to tell you that we could leave at once and that the carriages were waiting for us."

Xenia gave a little shiver.

This was what she had imagined would happen.

"I walked across the room to take you in my arms and tell you how much I was looking forward to our being alone," the King went on. "To my surprise, you turned your head away and said:

"'Really, István! I thought we had agreed to behave like civilised people!'"

He drew in his breath as if he remembered what a shock the words had been, then he continued:

"'What has happened?' I asked. 'Why do you speak like that?'

"'I cannot imagine why you thought I should want to go on a honeymoon,' you replied. 'I told you when we became engaged that while I would do what you wished in public, my private life was my own!'

"'Have you gone mad?' I enquired. 'And why are you talking like this after all we said to each other last night?'

"You shrugged your shoulders and walked to the window.

"'Let me make it clear,' you replied in a hard voice. 'I wish to stay in Molnár for the next few weeks, and nothing will make me go anywhere else!'

"I felt as if I must be in a nightmare," the King said.

There was a note in his voice which told Xenia he had not only been surprised but also deeply hurt.

Because she could not bear to think that he had suffered even for a moment, she put her arm round his neck and pressed her cheek against his.

"For a moment I could not think," he continued. "I just knew that something fantastic had happened, but my brain would not take it in. It was not you, and yet you looked as beautiful as ever. Your red hair glittered in the sunshine and your eyes were entrancingly green.

"'What has happened?' I asked again.

"'Nothing has happened,' you snapped. 'It is just

162

that you are changing the arrangements we made in Prussen. Send the carriages away and give orders that we shall be staying here in the Palace.'

"'And if I refuse?' I enquired.

"You turned round to the window and said:

"'Then you can go on your honeymoon by yourself. Why not take Elga with you?'

"I knew then that it was not you speaking. It was someone who looked like you and spoke like you, but . . ."

The King paused before he said:

"It flashed through my mind that you had a split personality, or that perhaps the stories of witch-craft in which a woman's body can be possessed by a demon were true."

Xenia kissed his cheek consolingly as he continued:

"There was a knock at the door, and, with what I thought was a note of relief in your voice, you called: 'Come in!' It was Count Gáspar.

"'Excuse me, Your Majesty,' he said, 'but the Dowager Grand Duchess is very anxious to have a word with you before she leaves.'

"Because I was so bewildered, so utterly stunned by what had happened," the King went on, "I followed the Count down the stairs to the Hall.

"'Forgive me for disturbing you, István,' the Grand Duchess said, 'but there is something I forgot to tell you yesterday which I feel is important.'

"'What is it?' I asked, not really interested.

"'I want you as soon as possible to take Johanna to see her grandfather.'

"'But why?' I asked.

"'Because King Constantine is not in good health and I suspect has not very long to live,' the Dowager Grand Duchess replied.

"I did not speak, finding it hard to think of anything but what had just occurred upstairs, and the Grand Duchess, misunderstanding my silence, said:

"'I know you have found him difficult in the past, István, but he has changed since he has been ill. In fact you will hardly believe it, but the other day he actually spoke of Lilla!'

"Again I did not reply, and she chattered on:

"'Perhaps you have forgotten who Lilla is, because no-one ever mentions her name. But she is in fact the twin sister of Johanna's mother.'

"'Twin sister?' I exclaimed.

"'But you must have been told,' the Grand Duchess said, 'that Dorottyn had a twin sister called Lilla, who ran away most reprehensibly with an Englishman, and a commoner at that. We were all forbidden ever to mention her, but I think that the King, now that he is dying, is softening in his attitude towards her.'

"'Twin sister!' I repeated.

"'They were identical,' my aunt said. 'Absolutely identical! No-one could tell them apart. But I always thought that Lilla was the softer, sweeter of the two.'

"She gave a little sigh.

"'I never knew what happened to her. I have often wondered if she had any children. I feel if she had a daughter she would look exactly like dear Johanna.'"

The King's arms tightened about Xenia.

"I knew then who you were and who I had married."

"Were you sure ... really sure?"

"I went back to Johanna and forced the truth from her," the King said. "She found it hard to be defiant and lie as she wished to do when I confronted her with what I was certain had happened."

"It was ... clever of you," Xenia murmured.

"I was fighting for everything that mattered to me in life," the King said simply.

He would have kissed her again but Xenia said quickly:

"Tell me the rest. I must ... know."

"I realised that I had to stop you from reaching

164

the border. Fortunately, Johanna was dressed and the Royal Train which you and I were to take on our honeymoon was waiting in the station."

He smiled before he added:

"We drove there at break-neck speed, stopping only at the Crown Hotel to pick up Lord Gratton."

"You took them both with you?" Xenia asked.

"I dragged them, if you like, into the train, and after telegraphing down the line to say I had to pass the slow train, we set off with really the minimum amount of delay."

"And Johanna agreed?"

"She had no alternative," the King replied, and for a moment his voice was hard. "But in case it should worry you, I have made her and Gratton as happy, or nearly as happy, as we intend to be."

"How have you done that?"

"I realised that while Johanna loved Gratton, what upset her was the idea of going into obscurity, and being of no importance, as your mother had been."

"So what have you arranged?" Xenia asked.

"I intend to make her the most talked about and the most famous Royal Personage in Europe," the King replied.

Xenia raised her head to look at him wide-eyed and he went on with a smile on his lips:

"All the world loves a lover, and a Princess who is prepared to give up a throne for the man she loves will be the focus of attention wherever she goes."

He paused before he said:

"In fact I think she will find herself of far more interest than a mere Queen of Luthenia!"

"But how can you do that? How?" Xenia asked.

"Simply by informing the Press. They can take the story from there."

"But you ... cannot! Think what they will say about ... you and ... me!"

"With Gratton's help we have trimmed the story

165

to our own ends," the King said. "Johanna decided to marry Lord Gratton, but because she felt so worried over the situation in Luthenia, you volunteered to take her place and convey to me the knowledge of what she intended to do."

His voice was slightly cynical as he said:

"Of course she wished me to be the first person to know where her real interests lay."

"Then what happened?" Xenia asked.

"We tell the truth," the King answered. "You and I fell in love at first sight, and in case there should be any family opposition because of your father's status as a commoner, we decided to get married before we told the world who you were."

Xenia gave a deep sigh.

"Oh, István . . . it is a . . . wonderful story!"

"It is a romantic tale that will be told and retold for many years to come," the King said. "Both you and Johanna will appear like heroines for the sacrifices you have made for love."

"I have sacrificed nothing," Xenia said quickly.

"But you were prepared to sacrifice me," the King answered, "and actually I am very angry that you should treat our love so lightly."

"Please . . . forgive . . . me," Xenia begged.

"Why did you not tell me after we were married?"

"I meant to . . . but I thought . . . you might be angry . . . and I so desperately wanted you . . . to kiss me . . . and to . . . love me."

He looked at her and his expression was very tender.

"I shall punish you, my precious, by making love to you until you cry for mercy, and never again will you dare to deceive me."

"I did not . . . wish to . . . do so . . . you know . . . that."

She hid her face against him before she whispered:

"If it had been the other way . . . round, I would willingly have . . . gone with you into . . . obscurity. I would have followed you . . . if you had wanted me, to the very ends of the . . . world."

The King held her very tightly against him.

"Do you suppose I do not know that?" he asked. "Our love for each other, my precious, is so great, so overwhelming, that we can neither of us be complete unless we are together."

He kissed her on the forehead, then set her on her feet and rose from the chair in which he had been sitting.

"I have a lot to say to you and a lot more explanations to hear," he said, "but we have our honeymoon ahead of us, and the carriages are waiting."

Xenia looked up at him, her eyes suddenly alight.

"Where are we going?" she asked and knew the answer.

"To my Castle in the mountains," the King replied. "We are going to be alone there, my darling, really alone, so that I can show you how much our love means and how it will be impossible for us ever to lose each other again."

He looked into her eyes, and as she saw the fire in his, she knew what he was wanting and she felt again the little flickering flames he had awakened in her last night.

"I shall never lose you," the King said. "That is one thing about which you may be absolutely sure. I know now, if I did not know it before, that it is impossible to live without you."

The happiness in Xenia's eyes seemed to light the whole room and he thought that no woman could look more beautiful or more radiant.

Then with an effort, as if he was afraid to touch her, he said:

"We are leaving, my lovely one, but there is one thing I must do first."

167

"What is that?"

"Arrange to tell the world what has happened! Then we can forget everything except ourselves."

"How do you intend to do that?" Xenia asked, curious.

The King did not answer. Instead, he walked across the room and pulled open the door.

"Horváth!" he called, and the Count appeared.

"Is that reporter still hanging about who tried to speak to me when we arrived?"

"Yes, Sire," the Count replied. "He is making a sketch of Your Majesty for his newspaper, and frankly, I think he is rather talented."

"Show him in," the King commanded. "I intend to make him the most important young reporter in Europe, and he will certainly end up a rich man."

The Count look astonished, but the King merely said: "Fetch him!" and turned back to Xenia.

She was looking at him with such an expression of love in her eyes that he merely held out his arms.

She ran to him.

"Is it . . . true, really true, István . . . that I can stay with you and . . . love you forever?"

"It is true, my beautiful darling," he said, pulling her closely against him.

"I . . . thought that, like Cinderella . . . midnight had struck and I was . . . back where I started . . . alone."

"Midnight has struck," the King replied, "but it is merely to herald another day. Our day, my darling, which will never be long enough for me."

He bent his head and kissed her as he spoke, and she felt that once again he carried her up to Heaven, where they had been last night.

"I love you! Oh . . . darling . . . wonderful István . . . I love you!" she murmured against his lips.

She felt the fierce passion of them exciting her as she excited him and drew closer still. . . .

Neither of them heard the door open, but an ob-

scure young reporter from a local newspaper was
able, after what he had seen, to draw a Royal em-
brace that was to be reproduced in every newspaper
in the world!

ABOUT THE AUTHOR

BARBARA CARTLAND, the world's most famous romantic novelist, who is also an historian, playwright, lecturer,
political speaker and television personality, has now written over 200 books. She has also had many historical
works published and has written four autobiographies as
well as the biographies of her mother and that of her
brother Ronald Cartland, who was the first Member of
Parliament to be killed in the last war. This book has a
preface by Sir Winston Churchill. Barbara Cartland has
sold 80 million books over the world, more than half of
these in the U.S.A. She broke the world record in 1975 by
writing twenty books, and her own record in 1976 with
twenty-one. In private life, Barbara Cartland, who is a
Dame of the Order of St. John of Jerusalem, has fought
for better conditions and salaries for Midwives and Nurses.
As President of the Royal College of Midwives (Hert-
fordshire Branch), she has been invested with the first
Badge of Office ever given in Great Britain, which was
subscribed to by the Midwives themselves. She has also
championed the cause for old people and founded the first
Romany Gypsy Camp in the world. Barbara Cartland is
deeply interested in Vitamin Therapy and is President of
the British National Association for Health.